Paolo Dune

THE DEVIL'S REASONS

Is it possible to defend the devil against the charge of
having damned the world?

A theological-judicial novel

Youcanprint *Self-Publishing*

Title | The Devil's reasons
Original title| L'attenuante 666 – Le ragioni del Diavolo
Author | Paolo Dune

ISBN | 978-88-27831-66-3

Youcanprint Self-Publishing
Via Roma, 73 - 73039 Tricase (LE) - Italy
www.youcanprint.it info@youcanprint.it
Facebook: facebook.com/youcanprint.it
Twitter: twitter.com/youcanprintit

The accuser of our brothers has been thrown down,
who accuses them day and night before our God

Revelation 12:10

An apology for the devil: it must be remembered that
we have heard one side of the case.
God has written all the books.

SAMUEL BUTLER

1

Traces of sulphur

> Then I saw an angel coming down from heaven, holding in his hand the key to the bottomless pit and a great chain. And he seized the dragon, that ancient serpent, who is the devil and Satan, and bound him for a thousand years, and threw him into the pit, and shut it and sealed it over him.

Revelation 20:1 et seq.

A bolt of lightning lit up the wet city streets turning the vague shadows of the night into ghostly forms, and a thunderclap followed him, making the buildings shake. Under the incessant rain, two police cars with their lights flashing stopped suddenly beneath the La Fourche underground railway signs, in Paris, and a group of armed police officers emerged. The railway staff's alarm had arrived half an hour before, making quick intervention necessary.

"He looked like a drug addict" said the ticket seller, "pale, with dark circles under his eyes, but he had… he had those things on his forehead."

The policemen observed the images taken by the closed circuit television cameras. An individual was aimlessly wandering around the underground railway passages, badly-dressed, looking dirty and shabby. Something unusual could be seen peeping through his curly hair.

"It must be a trick…" the lieutenant said, "but just in case it isn't, let's be prepared for anything."

The group of policemen went down into the dimly-lit underground, where the air was cold and damp, in amidst the gaunt people who populated it, until they had identified the suspect.

They walked towards the lower level, where the pavement leading to Saint-Lazare was located.

"What's that on his forehead?" someone asked.

"Perhaps a malformation…" the lieutenant answered.

He was seen walking near the railway lines, as a train arrived, shaking the tunnel. He didn't seem to want to leave and stood still on the platform, in the wind, watching the train as it stopped and a few passengers getting on and off. In the end, he walked along behind a girl who was headed for the exit.

The policemen monitored him at a distance, as his footsteps echoed towards the exit. When they heard the girl scream from the top of the long moving staircase, they intervened.

"Stop right there!" they warned him.

The individual turned towards them and fluorescent reflections could be seen coming from his shining eyes. There were two protuberances sticking out of his forehead, like horns, and from his mouth a forked tongue.

Everyone's blood ran cold.

With a jarring sound, the individual vomited an acidic liquid over some of the policemen as he leapt onto the wall, sticking to it like a spider, and ran across the ceiling.

Gripped by terror, the men opened fire, emptying their guns onto the shadow that ran up above them, until an explosion of sparks on an electrical cable caused a blackout, leaving the place in darkness.

The creature continued to move, leaving fiery footprints, until he reached the train platform again. He jumped onto the tracks and ran into the mouth of the tunnel. A moment later, a long, piercing squealing of brakes was heard, followed by a thud, a crash and the sound of metal.

As it derailed, making a deafening noise, the last underground train careened out of the tunnel, ramming into the platform.

A little way down, slumped on the tracks and unconscious, the outline of the fugitive could be seen.

The criminal act made his immediate arrest possible.

∽ ∽ ∽

A couple of hours later, as the rain continued to fall on the city, a barrage of telephone calls flooded the French government's emergency line, alerting the political leaders. In a state of shock, the Minister of Defence entered the French President's office at the Élysée Palace.

"I got here as quickly as I could" he said, adjusting his tie.

Another minister, seated on a sofa in the dim light, shook his head, muttering: *"Mon Dieu, Mon Dieu..."*

The president of the French Republic, Jacques Renard, was standing in front of the window, staring into the darkness of the city, wet from the downpour.

"Come and sit by the fire" he said absently, pointing at an armchair near the fireplace.

"So, what is it all about?" he asked the other man. "Have we captured a terrorist?"

He replied, somewhat confused: *"Isaiah,* chapter 14: "Is this the man who made the earth tremble, who shook kingdoms, who made the world like a desert and overthrew its cities, who did not let his prisoners go home?".

"What does that mean?"

"Do you believe in transcendence?"

"In transcendence?"

"I didn't believe in it until now."

"What do you mean?"

"You'll understand when you see it."

"See it?"

"Thin, bad-smelling, inhuman. It seems like there are some sulphurous springs down there."

"A demon? *Que diable*, it's impossible!" The minister seemed to waver when faced with this news. He wiped his forehead with a handkerchief, while President Renard, deep in thought, walked silently over to his desk. In so many years of politics, he had never had to deal with an emergency like this one and even the slightest mistake could be fatal for him.

"Well, we need to alert governments worldwide", the minister continued, "and also the Vatican: if the story were to be true, we would have material proof of the existence of metaphysics!"

"There's no hurry" the President replied, lighting a cigar and inhaling slowly. "He's really just small-fry."

"What?"

He blew cigar smoke into the air. "He's just a young demon who had never come to Earth until now. We might be able to get to his boss."

"You want to capture... Satan?" the minister exclaimed. "*C'est folie!*"

"It's the wisest thing to do, though" he replied, his eyes shining through the smoke, "this devil can lead us to the heart of evil."

"Do you want to organize a squad and send it... to Hell?"

"We need to be in agreement with the executive branch. In the meantime, it would be better not to inform anyone."

"But the other governments have a right to know... the devil is a global threat!"

"If we succeed in catching him, our country will get important recognition. Providence has offered us this opportunity and we can't squander it; we must act cautiously."

The third man present, the Minister of Internal Affairs, continued to mumble to himself in a corner: *"Mon Dieu, mon Dieu…"*

∽∽∽

The next day, the secret services subjected the prisoner to a series of interrogations. With his dark eyes and scarred face, the demon brandished an air of indifference. Nevertheless, the investigators thought they could make him cave. Blood samples were taken, in order to analyse his genetic structure and various elements of compatibility with species of extinct primates were found.

"He could be an ancestor of ours" a scientist suggested, "an example of a species unknown to date, the missing link between *Homo sapiens* and the first hominids."

Someone would win a Nobel prize with research carried out on the devil.

Suddenly, after days of isolation, the creature asked to be heard. He spoke a confused mixture of various languages, but was able to make himself understood.

"You're crazy if you're trying to find *Satán*; it is he who is looking for you!"

"Does a being named Satan really exist?"

"He's here, on Earth. He is invisible and he moves among men, guiding them for his own purposes, but I know his hiding places."

The prisoner decided to cooperate, in exchange for a guarantee of protection. The information provided made bilateral agreements between France and Germany necessary, so that a joint plan of attack could be prepared.

It was on the night of 31 October that military forces entered into action. Somewhere, the night of witches, Halloween, was being celebrated.

A large deployment of forces reached a hill on the outskirts of Berlin, in the centre of the Grunewald forest.

The Teufelsberg, the so-called "mountain of the devil", was a hill created artificially in the Post-war period out of rubbish left over from the war and debris from the bombings. An observation point had been built on its peak, as well as a radio station to accommodate spies during the Cold War and was then abandoned after the fall of the Berlin Wall.

Visiting the Teufelsberg was considered extremely dangerous and nobody dared go there.

Although black clouds were gathering in the sky, helicopters flew over the area, identifying a grey building with three large white balls on top of it, protected by a double barbed wire fence.

On the ground, a group of soldiers opened up a passage and began their climb to the top. This rugged land was covered in debris, sheets of metal, open manholes, old wreckage.

"Pay the utmost attention" the colonel ordered.

The soldiers advanced, noticing unusual sulphur vapours shining in the darkness and, on the ground, goat's hoof-prints leading along the winding trail. Crows were cawing and there was barking coming from the undergrowth. Someone swore they had seen the shape of a large animal, like a three-headed dragon, moving between the trees.

When a lightning bolt lit up the place, the building appeared, looking hostile: there were three dilapidated round structures, like gigantic golf balls. The outer wall was no longer there and it was possible to climb a worn-out flight of steps at the back. The colonel led the group along the path, being careful of the floor, which was missing in places, and of the open lift shaft, which was like a bottomless pit.

The soldiers walked close to the wall, as there was no railing, until they found themselves inside one of the domes, where every sound echoed noisily. From there, through the tatters of fabric flapping around in the wind, they got a glimpse of the town in the night-time panorama.

The torches ripped through the veil of darkness inside the building: there were no bedrooms, nor a kitchen or bathrooms. There was just an empty room welcoming them with an icy silence. The ceiling was hidden by spiderwebs, the floor was covered in dust and mould and mice were hiding in the corners. The soldiers were equipped with infrared glasses and followed other goat's hoof-prints that inexplicably wound around the walls and over the ceiling. Finally, on the other side of a metal door, they found a spiral staircase leading to the top floor. The officers approached cautiously. A few notes of classical music seemed to echo in the sighs of the wind and traces of sulphur soiled the steps.

In the tallest dome, a room appeared in the semi-darkness and it was much larger than it seemed from the outside. A gust of wind echoed in the stairwell and made the building sway, as a series of lightning bolts lit up the room intermittently: there were a few broken cable terminals, a wall clock that didn't work and a scratched mirror that only reflected the fragmented face of the moon.

The music that they could hear was coming from a gramophone in a corner of the room and, although there was no record on it, it was playing classical music.

"Ghosts!" the men exclaimed, feeling afraid. Some were unable to overcome the stress and went back downstairs, ending up falling into the stairwell. Someone recognized the music: *It's the Devil's Trill.*

"It's just your minds running away with you" the colonel assured them, restoring order.

Gripping their guns, the officers advanced on a creaking floor, until something frighteningly vivid suddenly appeared in the beams of light from the torches. They could see a human shape sitting on a black leather couch.

The man was wearing a white shirt, open over his chest, on which a crystal glass was balanced, and he had one arm bent over his face. He was motionless, as if he were dead; and the darkness made it hard to see his facial features. There was also a snake, coiled and hissing at the foot of the couch.

The colonel ordered the men to take their positions. Then a thunderclap shattered the glass and the figure on the couch awoke, saying an unintelligible word: "*Jhwh!*"

The policemen stepped back with their guns aimed at him and the small red laser lights from the guns wavered menacingly on the target.

Scrutinizing the visitors, the man's eyes shone like burning embers. "Visitors in Hell"

A circle of fire began to burn on the floor around the couch and its occupant. One of the policemen accidentally fired a shot and hit the target in the chest.

With a scream, the shadow writhed against the wall. The colonel warned: "Don't shoot!"

As the being collapsed before them, the officers hesitated. The creature slowly got up and looked at them. There was no wound on his chest. Opening his arms as if invoking someone or something, the flames around him seemed to answer by crackling.

"Satan!" the colonel exclaimed.

The soldiers opened fire and the entire building shook.

Growling fiercely, the prince of the underworld hurled several of them away and injured others. His shadow moved along the walls, grabbing hold of the policemen.

The helicopters were impotent, hovering around the building, watching the scene, as human torches fell out of the windows and then, in turn, were attacked by a swarm of bats.

After what seemed like forever, the being calmed his ferocity, as if yielding to a higher power. He fell, resigned, giving up the fight, as a few tranquilizer bullets reached his sides, weakening him. The circle of fire around him slowly went out.

Only when he fell to the ground and large metal handcuffs were locked around his wrists, the men present let out a triumphant cheer.

"I'm proud of you, lads" the colonel said.

The music from the gramophone stopped and a thunderclap shook the building, shattering other windows.

Evil had been captured.

∽ ∽ ∽

"I'm not convinced" said the penitent demon, after following the operation from the Ministry of Defence in Berlin. "Even if your electromagnetic interference had isolated him, it just seemed too easy."

"Easy?" said the colonel. "Dozens of injured, burnt, intoxicated men. Not to mention those bitten by the snakes or taken to hospital in a state of shock! And what will become of their souls?"

The demon did not reply.

Back at the Teufelsberg the soldiers spent all night exploring the building, discovering secret passages and deactivating mortal traps. In an underground room, they found a metal door from which intense heat was coming. Beyond the door, a narrow, winding staircase carved out of the rock led unnaturally downwards.

A word engraved on the wall seemed to be a warning:

HADES.

"The Greek Underworld..." someone said, "a passage for demons."

"A passage to the other world, a bridge over hell!"

They walked back, feeling afraid.

"The gates of Hell."

Going down those steps might turn out to be worse than any Vietnam. So the door was walled up and the demon's hideaway was seized. Hell was in isolation.

2

The great investigation

Gospel according to Matthew 5:39

The Vatican's marble cupola was being lit up by the sun in the east, when St. Peter's successor was abruptly awoken by the news. His personal secretary entered his bedroom, out of breath, and opened the purple curtains, letting the gentle light of dawn into the room.

"Holiness", he said, "the prophecies of the *Apocalypse* are coming true: they have captured him! They've captured the Beast!"

"Cardinal Santelli? ..." Teomondo III asked sleepily, turning over beneath the sheets.

"No, Holiness, the rebel angel!"

"Who?"

"The theologians were right! Numerous signs predicting the apocalypse have occurred: wars, pestilence, famine. This is the final event. Now that we have captured Satan, we are at the final challenge!"

"Satan?! But I had just finished an encyclical..." the pope grumbled, throwing the covers aside and getting out of bed.

At that very moment, in the Dome of the Rock in Jerusalem, the light filtered through the stained glass windows of the Islamic temple, lighting up the mosaic of gold tiles covering the walls. When the imam, deep in prayer, was informed of what had happened, he was very distressed: "The materialization of Evil has a deep meaning. Hell has broken out of its chains and is coming up to Earth".

With unprecedented speed, the news of Satan's capture exploded in just a few hours all over the world, making the newspapers publish special editions:

INHUMAN CREATURE CAPTURED,

SATAN IS IN OUR HANDS,

LUCIFER'S SECOND FALL,

HUMANITY ON THE WAY TO REDEMPTION?

News flashes interrupted programmes being broadcast to announce: "Unknown creature captured during a military operation, possibly identifiable as the biblical devil, Satan, the prince of darkness. The event is one of unique importance. Is this a sign of the apocalypse?"

In his pure white dressing gown, walking at a fierce pace, Teomondo III entered the Vatican lounges where a steaming breakfast awaited him on the large table. Teomondo was a corpulent and determined man and was famous for having been a brilliant theatre actor when he was young, but he had no appetite that morning. The news that the devil had been captured had ruined a great many of his plans and had upset him considerably. A few months earlier, the conclave had entrusted the fate of the Church to him: the new Internet evangelizations and tax concessions had been the dominant topics of his programme.

As soon as they saw him, two cardinals, who were having a discussion, went over to him and kissed his jewelled ring. One was Camerlengo Santelli and the other was the secretary of State.

With a gesture of his hand, Teomondo dismissed the formalities: "Exactly what happened?"

The secretary hesitated: "It seems, Holiness, that they have captured the Devil... but we don't know the details".

"The Devil, *our* Devil?" he asked, incredulous. "How is that possible? And who was able to do something like that without alerting us?"

"It seems like the secret services must have intervened..."

"But we have informers everywhere; confessors, nuns and worshippers all over the world." the pope said, pointing his finger severely at the Camerlengo: "This capture will mean the governments' uncalled-for interference in spiritual matters and it could jeopardise relationships between the State and the Church!"

The other man nodded.

"How has public opinion reacted?"

The Camerlengo showed him a few newspapers: "They are all confused, Holiness. They believed that evil was a spiritual concept and they don't know how to explain this corporeality".

The pope sat on an armchair, browsing through the headlines. "Thousands of years of theology to reconsider."

Sounding worried, the secretary added: "The Church had been ignoring the figure of Satan for too long and worshippers had started to doubt his existence. Baudelaire warned us that the Devil's most cunning trick was to make men believe he didn't exist. But now his deception has been revealed! His capture marks retribution for the traditional positions".

"It may even determine an increase in vocation" the Camerlengo said, with optimism.

The Pope did not seem convinced: "Call the best demonologist and ask him to give a theological interpretation of the event. As for myself, prepare me a speech about Divine mercy for the next *Angelus*."

The Camerlengo took note, looking doubtful: "About mercy, Holiness?"

"We need to offer the world an image of reassuring normality. No press releases for now." He got up and went to leave.

"But Holiness," the secretary tried to reply, "apart from a few verses of the *Apocalypse* that hint at capturing the Devil, this event was clearly expected according to the prophecies... Perhaps we should give the worshippers a justification."

Teomondo was on the verge of saying something, but he changed his mind. It was not the right moment to reveal what was worrying him the most. He left without saying anything else.

The news of the Satan's capture created widespread anxiety and, while the atheists were perplexed about what had happened, the believers were distraught. The theologians discussed a possible crisis in the realm of darkness, and even the criminal world was alarmed: "If they have managed to arrest the Devil, nobody is safe."

In a Scottish castle in Edinburgh, the headquarters of the masonic Grand Lodge, the members of the organization reunited in a special session to listen to the Grand Master: "The clerical world is trying to reinforce its power by demonizing evil. We must avoid a fundamentalist drift".

Lastly, in a televised interview, the famous Hungarian exorcist father Cimor, appointed by the Vatican to study what had happened, illustrated the mystery of the devil's corporeality to an incredulous world.

"I have studied every aspect of the Devil - ancient, medieval and modern. I have traced him through the religions and demonologies of every population and even more through the history of mankind, hunting him out in the most remote corners of reality."

Cimor was the authoritative president of the International Association of Exorcists and was a thin, bald priest with an ashen complexion and deep-set eyes. He had been at the forefront of the battle against evil for years and had taken this event to heart. As soon as he was informed of the capture, he had torn his robes, sprinkled ash all over his head and then lay on the ground with his arms wide open in mystical prayer.

"Demons are spiritual creatures, but they are heavier than angels and take on a human form on earth" he said. "If God can take on a human form, they can do so even more, as they are more corruptible. Medieval chronicles are full of tales about their appearances. In the sixteenth-century *De praestigiis daemonum*, the demonologist, Johann Weyer, calculated the existence of 44,435,556 of them!"

Those listening were stunned.

"Demons live in an underground dimension parallel to ours, which can be reached via inter-dimensional passages that can be opened up with an adequate knowledge of the occult. They have retractable wings allowing them to fly at a low altitude; but their weight does not allow them to reach Heaven… They nourish themselves on the dark energy of the moon, but they also appreciate human cooking. They cannot die a natural death, but they can be killed: the most effective way is decapitation. Now, far away from the gates of Hell, the prince of darkness cannot return to his realm and cannot escape.

He is a prisoner here, in our world, in our time."

His words rang out like a dark prophecy, almost a threat to humanity.

∽∽∽

Amidst all the general bewilderment, the French President and the German Chancellor seemed to be the only ones who were not worried about this evil presence in the world. They liked the idea of executing the Devil in the public square, before the eyes of the entire world and, for the occasion, President Renard wanted to bring back the guillotine with the aim of preserving the Devil's head in a museum; the German leader preferred a traditional burning at the stake, followed by the scattering of his ashes in the wind. However, a group of animal rights supporters unexpectedly occupied the square in front of the European Parliament in Brussels, with banners, accusing the European governments of intolerance.

"The Devil belongs to a species that can throw light on our origins and we have no right to kill him."

Other international associations intervened in support of the bizarre initiative. Some scientists objected that it would be useful to study the Devil in order to identify the origin of evil. The issue spread elsewhere and a great deal of consensus was found, dividing public opinion and creating problems for the political leaders.

The German chancellor stormed into the French President's office. "The world has gone crazy!" he exclaimed. "They want to keep the Beast alive!"

His French colleague observed the German Chancellor's large body and round head, as he slowly inhaled his cigar smoke. "The world has always been mad" he said calmly from beneath his aquiline nose.

"But now we're exaggerating: we can't even demolish the Devil's headquarters in Berlin, because the Authority wants to turn it into a museum!

"Hands off Cain" Renard said distractedly.

"What?"

"Hands off Cain", the slogan of several civil rights movements."

"I've got nothing against Cain, but this is the Devil, it's much worse!" he said, scratching his forehead as he sank into an armchair.

The other man flipped through the calendar on the desk. "However, the European Parliamentary elections are not far off" he said, "and it would not be of any help if we have an excessively rigid attitude towards the Devil. Many constituents might identify with him."

"Are you joking?"

Renard leant forward: "It has taken thousands of years to capture him and it would be a pity to kill him without getting to know him in depth. What do you think about organizing... a trial?!"

"What?"

"A trial against Satan! "Eschatological-criminal" proceedings, at the end of which we will be able to execute him, and do it by the book."

"Putting the Devil on trial?"

"Evil will be facing charges, the Devil will be going before the bar, Hell will be standing trial. It will give us an excellent image abroad and we will have more time to study the creature."

Chancellor König mopped the sweat from his brow with a large handkerchief and reflected; waves of wrinkles marked his wide forehead. "It's not a bad idea at all," he concluded and his face brightened. "We would become the champions of contemporary democracy."

"And all within the law!" Renard said, his face lighting up too. "We could even broadcast the trial live worldwide and sell the copyright... We need to discuss this with our allies."

∽ ∽ ∽

The television news programmes were soon broadcasting a sequence of surprising news reports: "After frenetic intercontinental contacts, the other governments have accepted the French President's proposal to give the Devil a normal trial, and this news has triggered the imagination of the public. However, a great many people disagree: putting the Devil on trial means putting the certainty about evil at stake, which is one of life's few certainties, and not everyone is willing to confront him".

In order to develop an effective trial system, an international convention of jurists and politicians was called at the European Court of Human Rights in Strasbourg. Each participant intended to lay claim to putting the devil on trial in their own country. The solution of relying upon the International Court of Justice in the Hague for crimes against humanity was discarded. Rabbi Tariz, religious authority of the State of Israel, pointed out that the Devil was a biblical creature and should be put on trial in Jerusalem; however, the Palestinians were opposed to this, for fear that the evil being might desecrate the sacred places.

The president of the United States suggested the city of New York, pointing out that the "Big Apple" symbolized original sin.

To help resolve the international crisis, the United Nations intervened, recommending that the Devil be put on trial in the neutral territory of Switzerland. Despite considerable dissent, the suggestion was accepted and the international criminal court was promptly initiated.

The evening news announced that "The UN's Blue Helmets are supervising the initiation of the UN directive and at this very moment an army escort is taking the Devil to Switzerland, where he will be locked up in a maximum security prison. The Attorney General of the Republic, Erik Marduk, a highly-esteemed lawman, has given his assurance that the Devil will be treated like any other defendant and has entrusted the prosecution to Chief Attorney: Dr Bernard Louis."

Attorney Marduk's face and silver hair appeared on the television screen: "We will support the prosecution with all available proof and the religions can file a civil action in the proceedings".

The case was to be presided over by the black judge Tom Salomon, famous for having conducted the trials of illustrious figures. He had never committed himself to any religion and was considered agnostic and *super partes*. As soon as he had been appointed, he arranged for a pre-trial detention order and prepared an expedited hearing.

The human justice machine was set in motion.

ⴉ ⴉ ⴉ

"He fell to Earth like a comet," the public prosecutor, Bernard Louis, murmured looking through a thick wall of glass. Working alongside this tall, robust man with wavy brown hair and a large jaw, was Attorney General Marduk, who was smoking a pipe.

Beyond the glass wall, the Devil, Satan, was chained to a chair in the maximum security room, wearing a shiny muzzle made of lead and steel that hid part of his face. A yellowish glow coming from the swaying light on the ceiling cast shadowy stripes over his face.

"The first couple of human beings probably watched, powerless, his streak of fire in the sky," the public prosecutor continued.

"Are all the consequences of the event known?" the attorney asked.

Bernard sighed: "The impact was so great that the Earth's crust was broken and this caused the continents to shift. A layer of toxic gas was released as a result of the impact and it blocked out the sun, causing glaciation and the extinction of the dinosaurs… with incalculable scientific damage".

"Maybe science will also file a civil action" the attorney reflected optimistically.

The magistrate opened his arms: "And the virus of evil spread throughout the planet, infecting everyone. But now we have finally succeeded in isolating it! The Devil can no longer hide".

The armoured door opened noisily and the two men entered the cell where the creature being investigated awaited them in the centre, silently and with his head bowed. The public prosecutor approached him and pointed a light in his face.

"You will have to confess!" he exclaimed. "Who are you really? What is the reason for your existence? You are not as big as we thought... Who is behind you? Who has covered for you until now?"

Irritated by the light, the Devil shook his head and his shadow got bigger behind him. "Don't I have a right to a defence lawyer?" he asked in a raucous voice.

"A lawyer?" Louis asked sarcastically. "You will have one when the time comes; but if you don't decide to cooperate *I* will become your hell!" Bernard Louis was not the type of person to let himself be intimidated by the presence of a devil, especially when firmly chained to a chair.

"I don't work for anyone" the creature mumbled from beneath the mask, "I have always been… independent."

"Do you want us to believe that you alone created all the evil in the world? Who helped you? Who are you protecting?"

Satan admitted faintly: "I received a certain amount of help from men…"

"The Freemasons? I want their names!"

"Nobody would believe me..."

The magistrate banged his fist on the table and began to walk around him exasperated: "You are bluffing! Who are you trying to scare? I'm not God you know! *I* do not forgive!"

Dead silence followed. The accused, who was still under the effects of sedation, kept his head hanging down and Louis then stood in front of him: "If you don't want to cooperate, we'll see you in court, where the penalty I obtain will serve as an example: it will be your head!"

He ordered the policemen to take him away and they grabbed hold of Satan, lifted him up out of the chair and took him back to his cell. He did not put up a fight.

"He won't talk," said the attorney general, who had been sitting in the corner.

"Perhaps," Louis reflected, rubbing his large jaw.

"In my opinion, he has no accomplices, no instigators. He is responsible for everything. And this simplifies things; it means that we have the situation perfectly under control."

Bernard muttered to himself, perplexed.

"Prepare yourself for the trial, Louis" his boss concluded, adjusting his tie. "I will prepare myself for public opinion!"

While a light rain fell on the city, inside the congress building on the Zurich lakefront, before dozens of television cameras, the attorney general answered questions put to him by journalists from every corner of the world, for the most important press conference held in the last few thousand years.

Scientists, religious people, pilgrims and simple onlookers had come into town to witness the event.

"Is putting the Devil on trial in Zurich a political choice?" the journalists immediately asked.

"No", Erik Marduk replied, hiding his satisfaction, "We simply implemented the UN resolution."

"Is it true that the Vatican had asked for his extradition, but it was denied for reasons of protection of civil liberties, for the fear of a new Inquisition?"

"No comment, I'm sorry."

"Will this excessive attention to the protection of civil liberties not be a pretext for some European governments to try to earn international prestige?"

"We are simply enforcing the law."

"When is the trial going to take place?"

"Very soon."

"And who will defend the Devil?"

"So far, the public defenders are conscientious objectors…"

The conference was interrupted when several Jehovah's witnesses appeared and tried to get through the gates, announcing: "The end of the world is nigh, the Beast is among us! Listen to horns of judgement day! Repent!"

News of the event had spread everywhere with an apocalyptic rumble.

3

The angel's advocate

But who are you, O man, to answer back to God?

Romans 9:20

Accompanied by two figures similar to himself, a man in a dark suit entered the law firm of a famous lawyer at the Bar of London in Queen Victoria Street. Young lawyers and trainees moved from one elegant, sombre room to the next with dossiers and documents. After looking around, the three men went over to the desk, where they were greeted by a young secretary: "Do you gentlemen have an appointment?"

"My name is Yorgo Mirakis," said the man with the beard, introducing himself.

The secretary opened her eyes wide and examined the middle aged man through her thick glasses. He had a black beard, long hair held back in a plait and a small scar on his cheek.

"I am the representative of the Luciferian sects: the Church of Satan, the Temple of Set and the Fraternitas Saturni. The lawyer, Mr Valance, is expecting me."

"Oh, of course," the secretary said, lifting the receiver. "Mr Valance, your client is here... yes, alright, I'll let him in. Please come with me," she said to the guest.

He gave her an icy look and followed her towards the office, while the other two men remained in the waiting room. The woman shuddered: she had heard about the satanic priest Mirakis. They said he was the head of fanatical Devil worshippers, necrophiliacs and perverts and she didn't like it one bit.

After a long talk, the door of the lawyer's office opened again and the man walked out. His expression was still menacing but there was now a slight hint of satisfaction on his face. He said goodbye to the secretary coldly and left with his two companions.

The woman smelt trouble.

Silent streaks of lightening in the distance lit up the dark late-November sky as the lawyer, Nick Valance, reached Horgen, a town on the outskirts of Zurich, to enter the massive prison of Bezirksgebäude. With a great many precautions, he was led into the maximum security area, where a series of highly-sophisticated electronic systems protected its occupants from the rest of the world.

Nick Valance was a tall, thin man, with brown hair, slightly greying at the temples, and a thin moustache, wearing a nut-brown coloured suit. As he went down to the basement floors in the armoured lift, escorted by two armed guards, he thought about the choice he had made when he agreed to take on the Devil's defence. His wife had strongly discouraged him, but he never listened to his wife's advice.

Valance was one of the United Kingdom's most highly-esteemed criminal lawyers and his eloquence had echoed through countless courtrooms. No one was more suited to defending this unique defendant, even though he had no idea about how he would organise his defence.

Located at the end of a long corridor, the suspect's cell was protected by electrified steel bars and a bullet-proof glass wall, as well as several crucifixes on the walls. The agents advised the lawyer not to get too close and to speak to him via a special microphone.

A strange mist lingered in the room, blurring its edges. But the Devil was there, lying on a small bed in the corner, wearing grey pyjamas, with his face in shadow.

When he saw the new arrival, he roused from his thoughts and scrutinized the elegant guest's apparel, raising one eyebrow.

"The devil's advocate?" he asked.

"They have called me that too," Nick confirmed.

The suspect muttered something in an unknown language and lay down again. He had a strange accent, as if he came from many different places but none in particular.

"I'm your lawyer," Nick continued "and I will defend you during the trial."

The Devil didn't speak right away and his facial features were still hard to distinguish. "A trial will not be sufficient to settle the score between mankind and Hell. Why did you accept?"

"Someone had to do it," Valance said, justifying himself. "The public defenders refused on ethical grounds and a satanic sect engaged me. Do you know Mr Yorgo Mirakis? He says he's a worshipper of yours."

"… A follower who evokes me far too often."

"Plus," said the lawyer, smiling, "I'm fascinated by challenges."

Mixing together various languages, Satan mumbled, "This is merely a farce, to absolve the magistrates, the jurors and the whole world… and I am a suitable element of contrast." He sat still for a few moments, as if he were deciding what to do, and then he pulled himself up and sat on the edge of the bed. As soon as the fog began to clear, the light lit up his face and Nick was able to observe him. He instilled unease, although his appearance was anything but lacking in charm. He was robust, with jet black hair over his shoulders, dark eyes, arched eyebrows and an angular face;

he had a pointed black goatee beard on his chin, framing his mouth.

He resembled the classic iconographic image.

"The Devil is not as terrible as he is depicted to be," the lawyer stated.

"He was depicted that way by man" the Devil replied.

"That might positively influence the jury, but of course this is the most demanding legal case of all time."

The Devil sniggered: "Don't be tempted by futile hopes, man. Do you think you have any hope of winning? Humanity has always shunned me, loathed me, and it's quite surprising that I wasn't executed immediately."

"Did they read you your rights when you were arrested?"

"I have never had any rights."

"Did they let you call someone?"

"In Hell?"

Nick had got up from his seat and was walking up and down in front of the glass wall. "We need to find something… What were you doing in that building in Berlin?"

The Devil seemed to dodge the question: "I own numerous dwellings in your world. And I would never have been captured if I had not been betrayed by one of my demons".

"Tell me about what happened."

"There was a tip off. Zepar, a mediocre apprentice of the third circle of hell, who had been recently appointed to external assignments, deserted."

"So, one of your demons betrayed you? What type of assignments had he been given?"

"They involved going to Earth and tempting humans. But he was awkward... and he was destined to return as a quarryman."

"Unfortunately this is a trump card for the prosecution."

The Devil shrugged with indifference.

"… You know what?" Nick added, observing him. "I had never seen a devil before. I didn't think you were corporeal."

"We are when we're on Earth. The Creator made us physical as a punishment," he said sarcastically, "and because of our weight, we fell from the clouds."

The lawyer pondered over the situation, as the prisoner stared at him, and then he approached him. "You will have to tell me everything, Mr Satan. I will need to know every detail of your life. That is the only way we can hope for something."

A strange laugh left the prisoner's lips as he, in turn, came closer to the lawyer. "I come from heights where no fantasy has ever flown; I know underworlds where no nightmare has ever been. I have endless things to tell you, man, but you will have to pluck up all of your courage to listen to them."

∽∽∽

The news of Nick Valance becoming the Devil's defence lawyer spread throughout the world, shocking conformists and alarming the political world. In a special meeting in Brussels, the heads of state analysed the situation, expressing their concerns.

"Do you think he might create problems for us?" the German chancellor asked.

The English prime minister, Lady Fillingham, who had just arrived from London, hesitated. In spite of her frail appearance, she was a sophisticated and authoritative woman.

"Nick Valance is one of the best criminal lawyers in the United Kingdom. He has pleaded numerous cases at home and abroad, in which he was brilliantly successful."

"He's just a lawyer," said the French president, Renard. "He can't perform miracles. Besides," he added "trying to prove the Devil's innocence is what we call *probatio diabolica* in courtroom jargon... it's an impossible feat. Valance only accepted because he wants publicity."

"Valance doesn't need publicity," Lady Fillingham pointed out, "and he doesn't accept cases if he doesn't intend to win them. We mustn't underestimate him."

"More importantly," chancellor König chimed in again, wiping his brow, "isn't there a risk that the accused might escape?"

"Our prisons are the best," the Swiss prime minister assured everyone. "Even God might find it hard to escape from there."

"And what about the trial? How can we guarantee public order around the courtroom?"

"We are building an underground tunnel, a supervised passage, which will allow us to move the Devil from the prison to the Palace of Justice without creating any chaos. The government will spare no expense."

President Renard lit a cigar, inhaling slowly. "I think that Valance's advocacy is the ideal solution." His eyes darted towards the astonished listeners. "If the Devil were to be defended by an inexpert lawyer we could be accused of partiality and that would cast doubt on the sentence. Instead, the intervention of an authoritative lawyer will not arouse any suspicion, thus making the sentence completely credible."

"Are you convinced of that?"

"Of course. Valance will be an excellent alibi, the Trojan Horse of our triumph!"

The others slowly approved... and then did so with more determination.

The "Lucifer case" was destined to become a worldwide event and, at that time, nobody could have imagined the consequences that it would lead to.

∽ ∽ ∽

Nick Valance was awoken early in the morning by a phone call from his wife calling from London, who wanted to join him in Switzerland. He convinced her to stay at home until the end of the trial: he wouldn't have felt free to act with his wife present and it could also be dangerous.

After a quick breakfast, he went to the law firm placed at his disposal by the Swiss Law Society, which was a top floor apartment in the Weinplatz, in front of the river Limmat. He had called a meeting with his staff of collaborators, informers and trainees, to ask them for help, even though he knew that his decision to accept the case had not aroused any enthusiasm.

In the furnished apartment filled with international codes and books, the lawyer examined the perplexed faces of the people who had been by his side in so many battles.

"I have never believed in the Devil, you know, and I don't think I believe in him even now. However, I have decided to defend him. If any of you do not want to follow me in this case, I will understand, but those who remain must offer me their serious and determined help."

They looked at each other undecided, until a young trainee got up, "I'm sorry Mr Valance, but I can't justify evil".

"There is a fine line between law and ethics and you are crossing it," said another.

"We all have family," a young man confided. "How can we go against God?"

At the back of the room, the detective, Moroni, threw away his cigarette end. "I'm with you, boss! When I was young, my girlfriend left me to become a nun and broke my heart. I've never liked those people ever since".

Frank Moroni was an Italian-American with a stiff face furrowed by a web of wrinkles. He was abrupt, always wore a shabby raincoat and had been working with Valance for many years.

The lawyer gave him a hint of a smile, "It isn't about liking or disliking, but about professionalism. Will you be able to rise above every form of prejudice in dealing with a case like this?

Sceptical glances were exchanged in silence.

"But do you believe that the Devil is innocent?" someone asked.

"Innocent or guilty, my job is to defend him."

Someone nodded, while others shook their heads. Then the secretary, Linda, got up and went to sit next to the lawyer. A resolute expression suddenly appeared on her timid face. After talking a great deal, the others got up and walked towards the exit, making no comments as they left in silence. The lawyer nodded ruefully. Every colleague that left felt like a subtle wound. Even old Benjamin, who had been his partner and friend for years, muttered something, sounding disgruntled, "I always thought that your presumption would lead you astray one day, my boy… and that day has arrived! The further you push yourself into this case, the more you will find yourself lost… and to defend whom? The Devil! I really don't understand you." He left, muttering to himself.

Silence remained in the room, a loyal companion in so many of his choices. Nick looked gratefully at his secretary and at detective Moroni, who had both stayed with him. He needed much more help in a case like this, but he was going to have to settle for what he had. That same afternoon, he explained the situation and assigned the relative roles.

"I have never read any sacred books, so you need to get me the most important literature and news on the subject. What I'm interesting in knowing is: who is the Devil? Who created him? What has he done so far? What are his goals?"

They took note and got down to work. There was not much time and they needed to get busy.

4

Cell 666

> You say: "I am innocent". Behold, I will bring you to judgment for saying "I have not sinned".
>
> *Jeremiah* 2:35

The eyes of thousands of reverent worshippers followed the plane with the symbol of the Vatican on it, as it landed on the runway of Kloten airport in Zurich. A powerful man got off the aircraft, wrapped in a pure white ermine cape and wearing a skullcap on his head. He was accompanied by a group of Swiss guards in their traditional yellow, red and blue uniform, with helmet and armour, followed by chamberlains in dress uniform. Pope Teomondo III, Vicar of Christ, had rushed there after cancelling all of his official visits.

Just the day before, Protestant theologians had spread around an interpretation of the trial, referring to St Paul's prophecy when he announced, "Do you not know that we will judge the angels?"

A criminal trial was not exactly what theology expected, but the angel Lucifer was undoubtedly the "first angel", the first to be judged and, in the inscrutability of the design, the unmistakable divine touch was evident.

Taking the prophecy seriously, Teomondo wanted to participate in the event in person. A hint of gratification and satisfaction transpired on his face, along with a great deal of nervous tension. Behind him, the exorcist, father Cimor, appointed by the Vatican to assist him, moved cautiously.

The Pope refused to speak to the journalists and was received by the Swiss President and by the bishop of the city. That same afternoon he met the attorney general, Erik Marduk, who was enthusiastic about his coming.

"I'm happy to see you, Holiness. I have learned that you wish to bear witness at the trial. Your word will undoubtedly be decisive."

"I hope so, I hope so," he said wistfully, frowning at the same time. "We find ourselves faced with forces that go far beyond human experience and imagination and we need to be discerning. Is it true that it was the intervention of an informer that made it possible to capture the devil?"

"A fallen devil, a twist of Fate perhaps, a small demon who provided us the site of his boss's hideout."

The Pope wiped his forehead. "Evil is stronger than we thought. We must bless the places that have been contaminated," he said, turning to the magistrate: "Would it be possible to meet the accused before the trial?"

"Do you want to meet the Devil, Holiness?"

"I want to look into the eyes of the being that damned the world," said the Pope, breathing deeply. "I doubt I would be able to convert him, but I must try."

"You wish to convert the Devil?"

"Lucifer was once an angel," the Pope pointed out.

"Oh, well, in that case... I'll see what can be done," the attorney promised.

∽ ∽ ∽

Thunder resounded like a shouting in his head, while bolts of lightning mercilessly pierced his memory. It was afternoon and the Devil was asleep in his cell, but his rest was tormented by confused memories of the past.

Although thousands of years had gone by, his sleep always brought him the same nightmare: his fall from heaven.

With the uproar of war and shouts of the soldiers all around, God's lightning hit him right in the chest, burning his heart, and he felt his soul become heavy as it dried up. Thus, his relentless fall from the highest heights of the heaven to the little blue planet below him began. Upon contact with the Earth's atmosphere his wings burst into flame, his skin shrivelled and the Earth voraciously opened up beneath him, swallowing him up into a bottomless chasm. The fall of the rebel angel finally exploded in the centre of the planet, provoking the greatest cataclysm in history. A hell fire that was never spent.

Lucifer awoke with beads of sweat on his forehead and his hands tightly gripping his empty, silent chest.

A guard called out to him from beyond the glass wall: "Hey, you've got visitors, pal".

The demon slowly woke up, remembering that he was a prisoner, as always.

He perceived a hostile presence approaching him and there was a smell of holiness in the air, when a group of men appeared in front of the glass wall.

Pope Teomondo III was accompanied by the attorney general Marduk, the lawyer Nick Valance, who had asked to be present, and the exorcist father Cimor. Wearing a red velvet mozzetta cape and a papal tiara on his head, the Pope looked satisfied. No religious leader had ever dared to go this far and if he were successful in his desperate attempt to convert the Devil, religious history would have to be rewritten. Father Cimor was the last of the group, enjoying this happy event; seeing the Devil powerless inside a cage had always been his dream.

Satan was surprised and raised an eyebrow, observing the two men of religion.

"The Vicar of God condescends to come down to this dungeon?" he asked indignantly.

The Pope stood his ground: "I came to see you, to look you in the face and observe the evil in the depths of your lost soul".

The devil got up, with a scornful look on his face. "I have witnessed the genesis of the world; I have waged war against the Almighty, I have led armies and I have governed the infernal underworlds. Now a group of mortals expects to judge me?"

The Pope took a step forward: "You sang your own praises before the Supreme one, Lucifer. That is why you fell from the clouds. You had a corner of heaven, but it wasn't enough: you wanted everything! You expected glory that was not yours".

Father Cimor intervened, taking out a little bottle of Holy Water and a silver crucifix with pointed ends, which he had used in the past when facing infernal creatures. "I have waited for this moment for a long time. The good Lord has brought you to me."

He threw the holy water onto the glass and began an exorcism ritual. Before the lawyer's astonished eyes, he knelt down and got up again whispering invocations: "*Tenebrarum filius, umanitatis seductor, innocentium persecutor...*"

The water sizzled on the glass.

Valance had to intervene. "This is not proper behaviour. You are harassing my client. Please stop or I will be forced to lodge a formal complaint".

"For the salvation of the world this creature must be silent," Cimor exclaimed.

"Be silent?" Satan repeated. "You have always been obstinate about this."

Cimor approached the glass holding the cross. "What do you mean?"

"A mediocre man who has found superiority in fanaticism," the Devil mocked. "Do you think you can turn off the darkness?"

Hatred and resentment accumulated through decades of rivalry came face to face, separated merely by a layer of glass.

"*Cave Deum, Lucyfer!* Repudiate yourself" Cimor pointed at him.

The Devil put his hands on the glass with a sardonic smile. The glass became red-hot and there was a short circuit in the system. A few sparks exploded upwards and the neon lights on the ceiling shattered, causing splinters of glass to rain down over everyone present.

Several fragments of glass hit the exorcist in the face and he put his hands over one eye.

The security services intervened, while a sudden blackout in the cell hid its occupant.

∽∽∽

A few hours later, the dramatic news had hit the headlines:

THE DEVIL INJURES AN EXORCIST IN ONE EYE,
EXORCIST HALF BLINDED BY THE DEVIL,
FATHER CIMOR LOSES AN EYE DURING HIS
ENCOUNTER WITH SATAN.

The theologians immediately referred to the prophecy of the *Apocalypse*, where it was announced, "Behold, the devil is about to throw some of you into prison, that you may be tested, and for ten days you will have tribulation".

Someone recalled the episode in which St Paul had blinded the sorcerer Elymas, who was in competition with him, and it was thought that this was a form of retaliation. The Pope reacted by formally excommunicating the Devil, something that had never been done before, and then thanked Providence for having protected him during the attack.

In his studio, Nick Valance could not avoid commenting on what had happened with the Satanist, Yorgo Mirakis.

"It was an awful gesture, which contributed to hastening a guilty verdict."

The other man tried to justify the behaviour: "Satan is an impulsive being".

"But what do we know about him? Who are we really defending?" Nick asked, unable to get a clear picture of his personality.

"Oh, Satan is very charismatic," the priest replied, livening up. "For us, he represents the rebellious force of nature against the oppression of the institutions and of conformism, but also the ability to build a rational world."

"An antagonist."

"The greatest antagonist! The devil's voice is the echo of the human conscience, of repressed instinct, of the most intimate and truest part of man."

"But after yesterday's episode, public opinion has already judged him," Valance concluded. "And I fear that we cannot expect any miracles."

At that moment, the secretary came in, waving a notebook. "Mr Valance, I've got the information you were looking for!" Her enthusiasm faded at the sight of the priest dressed in black. "It wasn't easy to convince the theologians to talk, but I got what I was after." she said, as Valance urged her to open the notebook. "So, the etymology of the word *devil* refers to the idea of "separator", "divider". His ancient name is Lucifer, meaning "bearer of light", but on Earth he is known as Satan, meaning "enemy" or Beelzebub, meaning "Lord of the flies". He has used various names throughout history: Ahriman for the Middle Eastern populations, Vetis for the Etruscans, Seth for the Egyptians,

Mouzouko for the Africans, Perkele for the Scandinavians, Jamen for the Indians. In the Hebrew texts, he is called Semyaza, Satanel, Mastema, Abaddon and Belial. Today he uses various names indifferently, like Iblis, "the proud one", for the Muslims, Mara for the Buddhists and Yama for the Asians ".

Detective Moroni exclaimed: "With all these pseudonyms he must have something to hide!"

"I have noticed that in some documents he is referred to as Satan, Lucifer and Beelzebub like three distinct entities" the girl observed.

"Oh, no" Yorgo Mirakis replied, "those are just three different aspects of the same person. When the angel fell to Earth, his personality grew, so that he could adapt to the environment. Satan is the great leader of hell, Beelzebub the torturer of souls, Lucifer the ancient rebel, the angel's ashes that hides inside them."

"A sort of Trinity…," Nick said.

Linda gave the priest a diffident glance before continuing: "In the beginning, Lucifer was a perfect angelic creature, God's first angel, the son of the dawn. According to tradition, he was a cherub appointed by God to be head of the "vigilantes", or guardians of the world. But then he committed the sin of pride: he was blinded by ambition and pride, making him wish to be similar to the Creator, and so he organized a rebellion to usurp heaven, causing a great war to break out. But the commander of the heavenly armies, archangel Michael, opposed his design and confronted him in the clouds, until Lucifer and his angels were defeated and exiled to Earth by God. It looks like they never stood trial".

"Summary justice?"

The woman read a passage from the book of *Isaiah*: "You said in your heart: 'I will ascend to heaven; above the stars of God I will set my throne on high; I will sit on the mount of assembly in the farthest reaches of the north; will ascend above the heights of the clouds; I will make myself like the Most High.' But you are brought down to Sheol, to the far reaches of the pit."

"Are the opinions on this story unanimous?"

"Well, according to the Koran, the sacred book of Islam, Lucifer was envious of the first man, who cheated him out of the privileges of being God's first creature. Since he refused to kneel before an inferior being, God punished him. "When we told the angels: 'Prostrate yourselves before Adam', they all prostrated themselves except for Iblis, who said, 'I should bow down before the one whom you created out of mud?"

"But we certainly have no eyewitnesses" Nick said. "Did someone have a motive to cover up this matter?"

"In any case, after his fall from the sky, Lucifer tried to make the whole of mankind unhappy, by leading them into temptation. His intentions are unknown, but we suspect that he wants to take revenge on Adam's descendants, by showing God that man is unworthy of his love. Perhaps he hopes to be reinstated."

"Undefined motive."

The girl added: "Today, the Devil lives in the Tartarus, or *Gehenna*, the deepest region of Hell, and his number, whatever it might mean, is 666".

The lawyer nodded: "And what news do we have about God?"

"Oh, very little unfortunately." Linda said, still flipping through the notebook: "His real name is unknown. He goes by Yahweh or *Jhwh*, an unpronounceable word that means "He who I am". he lives in the Seventh Heaven along with the angels, the saints and the prophets. But his intentions and designs are unknown. All we know is that he wants to save us".

"Save us from what?"

"Well, from what he would do to us if we were to reject him."

Valance walked around the room, looking perplexed, with his hands behind his back. A sudden heavy shower had darkened the sky and large drops of rain streaked the window panes. "It's insufficient for formulating a defence. We need more details... and there is only one being who can give them to us."

A thunderclap echoed outside.

∽∽∽

Lucifer's cell had been further fortified with new electronic systems, but when Nick went to see its occupant, he asked to enter the cell in order to have a private conversation.

"Are you joking?!" the prison warden objected. "After what happened to father Cimor, God only knows what else that prisoner might do."

"I need to speak to my client in private for preliminary investigation requirements."

"Do you not fear for your safety?"

"I'm quite sure he will not harm me, as I'm his only hope."

"But he could possess you and escape with your involuntary complicity."

"You can have your officers watch over me."

Valance's persistence prevailed and, later on, the door of cell 666 was opened to the lawyer. Armed policemen watched him enter the room and sit on a chair, after closing the door behind him.

Inside the cell, a smell of sulphur filled the air and the temperature was low. Numerous threatening letters were piled up on the table, but there were also some letters of appreciation and solidarity sent by admirers from various parts of the world. However, none of them had been opened.

Satan was lying motionless on the small bed in the corner, as if he were dead. Valance coughed politely, awakening him from his nightmares.

"Oh, Mr Valance. Have they arrested you as well?" he asked.

"I came to speak to you, Lucifer. You need to tell me anything you know that might be useful for the trial. The preliminary hearing is in a few days and we need to prepare a coherent defence."

"My name is Satan," he specified. "Lucifer is the name of an angel who no longer exists."

Valance bowed his head respectfully. "Please excuse me."

When the prisoner stared at the listener, his eyes were lifeless, like dark pools that no sun could brighten.

"Nothing will be able to save me. You are just wasting your time."

"It also depends on you."

The Devil turned his back on his guest: "I am nothingness, absolute negativity, the evil that mankind has always been fighting".

"In a rule of law, the jury must only answer to the law."

"Do you believe in the law, Mr Valance?"

Valance looked away and then answered: "We don't have much time on our hands".

"What do you want to know?"

«First of all, why did you harm father Cimor? What is the meaning of the words you exchanged before that? Had you already met each other?"

The Devil did not answer and began to walk around the room with his hands crossed on his chest. Behind him, his shadow moved unnaturally.

"I will tell you something," he said, giving Valance a piercing look. "I had encountered Cimor several times in the past, but I had never met the Pope up until now. Their presence here means that the Holy See does not appreciate my testimony. They probably fear that I might shed light on poorly defined theological issues," the Devil said, walking towards him. "The thing that makes a dogma credible is its absolute incomprehensibility. Revealing it means shattering the aura of mystery on which it is founded. Mystery clouds the waters to make them look deeper; men will kneel down when faced with the indecipherable, but never before something that they can measure up to".

"Do you think this is the reason for the Church's hostility?"

"If religions become rational, that will be the end of them."

"And could this be useful to us in the trial?"

"You tell me."

Nick Valance took out a small voice recorder and got ready to take notes.

"First of all, why don't we address each other on a first-name basis?" the prisoner suggested with a knowing smile.

"I am not used to using confidential tones with my clients," Nick replied. "Now, can we please begin?"

About two hours later, after a long talk, Nick Valance left the cell, looking pale but satisfied. The policemen searched him and the chaplain blessed him.

"You can leave now, Mr Valance," said the prison warden. "Did you get the answers you were looking for?"

Nick smiled: "The prisoner suggested some evidence to me, *probatio diabolica*".

∽ ∽ ∽

The preliminary hearing took place a few days later behind closed doors and, as predicted, it was brief. In the courtroom of the Kantonales Gerichtsgebäude, the Palace of Justice in Zurich, the lawyer asked for the accused to be released on the grounds of a lack of evidence, underlining that Satan's original sins, dating back thousands of years, were barred by the statute of limitations and he objected to the court's lack of jurisdiction, as the accused was an unearthly being. However, his position was not taken into consideration: the statute of limitations was excluded, based on the seriousness of the indictments, and human jurisdiction was deemed legitimate based on the accused's constant activity on Earth.

Twisting a ringlet of his white wig around his finger, judge Salomon looked the lawyer and the public prosecutor up and down without hiding his concerns. Fate had chosen him, a black magistrate, to judge the evil of the world, and the press had put a lot of emphasis on this. Not only did the most demanding case in the history of law rest on the elderly man's shoulders, but so did an enormous moral responsibility.

Sighing, he cautioned the two sides: "I suffer from high blood pressure, gentlemen, and I'm supposed to be retiring in the coming spring. My desire is to retire to a house by the lake and spend my old age with a fishing rod in my hand. Therefore, the trial must take place in the proper manner: the public prosecutor must formulate precise charges and the defence must keep to the usual procedure. Nothing theatrical, nor any miracles. If you have no further questions, I will send the case to trial".

The judge's wooden mallet struck the bench with a dull thud.

Good and Evil, the Heavens and the Underworld, were destined to confront each other and they would be doing it on Earth, in human history.

As he left the courtroom, Valance was approached by a worried-looking Yorgo Mirakis. "How did it go, Mr Valance?"

"They're going to try him," Nick explained. "We will defend ourselves during the hearing."

"Is there something I can do?"

"Apart from giving me an advance on the expenses?" Nick smiled. "Well, I suppose you could pray."

5

The days of judgement

Gospel according to Matthew 7:1-2

When the producer began the countdown, there was a lot of tension among the operating crew. After long negotiations, the television had obtained the right to be present and to film the initial phases live. The programme was widely publicised and anxiously awaited. Its title was "The universal trial" and it was destined to become the most highly-viewed, discussed, studied, praised, criticized television production ever to be broadcast in the history of television. Even the liturgy of entertainment demanded veneration.

There was a sign and the red light came on. The live show opened with a screenshot from above of the courtroom packed with people. The set-up had been organized by carefully-chosen European set designers: marble columns, crystal chandeliers, velvet armchairs, large windows, international flags and the golden scales, the symbol of justice, dominating the back of the room. A gallery had been built especially for ticket-payers.

Filmed close up by the television cameras, the American journalist Sophia Madlane began, "Today marks the start of the most important trial in history, second only to that against Jesus. The accused is the prince of darkness, the Lord of the flies, the great slanderer and the tempter par excellence, the creator of all the evil in the world.. in one word, the Devil. When the world had forgotten him, Lucifer re-emerged to undermine its certainties. From being the great accuser of man with God, today he has become the great accused. As theologians have observed, as well as St Paul's prophecy, according to which humans would one day judge the angels, the book of *Revelation* is also coming true: it announces the capture and imprisonment of the Devil for a thousand years..."

The accused sat inside a solid steel cage and the journalists had tried to approach him in vain. The Swiss government had prohibited every form of interview in order to prevent the prisoner from sending messages to his accomplices in Hell. To prevent any attempts to lynch him, the Kantonales Gerichtsgebäude, the courthouse, was being protected by the United Nations peacekeepers. As the television cameras showed, the Hirschengraben and the roads parallel to it were closed to traffic, with road blocks and soldiers in anti-riot uniform.

The journalist continued: "The public prosecution is represented by the first attorney, Bernard Louis, assisted by his colleague Natalie Brinne, an expert in ecclesiastical law. Furthermore, the head of the satanic sects, Yorgo Mirakis, is present and will be held responsible for civil damages should the accused be sentenced. Now, the individual representatives of the religions are taking their places; it is the first time that representatives from so many different denominations have gathered under the same roof: Jews, Catholics, Orthodox, Protestants, among whom Lutherans, Anglicans and Calvinists... and then there are Muslims, Hindu, Buddhists, Shintoists and Confucians. The Shiite

Muslims have refused to participate, in protest against a trial that they describe as "an offence to divine justice".

The television cameras offered an evocative tracking shot of all the religious representatives in their traditional dress. Recognizable in the first few rows, was Pope Teomondo III, the Ecumenical Patriarch of Constantinople, the head rabbi Tariz, the Archbishop of Canterbury and the imam representing the Muslim congregations. An important absentee was the Buddhist Dalai Lama, who merely sent a telegramme of solidarity to his colleagues.

The journalist Sophia Madlane was well-known and popular with the public. She had been a news correspondent in the hottest areas of the world, she had investigated crimes of state and massacres that had gone unpunished and she had risked her life several times. She was determined and curious by nature and she loved her job because she loved looking for the truth, wherever it was. Now, before the legendary Biblical antagonist, she found herself involved in the most important journalistic case in human history.

While the television cameras filmed the audience, one of the paparazzi moving around the front rows succeeded in climbing over the fence and past the guards, reaching the Devil's cell, clutching his camera.

Unperturbed, Lucifer got up and crossed his arms over his head, making himself look like he had been sentenced to death: "Go ahead, shoot!"

There was a flash and a moment later the guards grabbed the man and promptly led him away.

The accused sniggered at that act of bravado; the photographer would have a dark picture and the device would be burnt inside. Films and digital systems could not capture images of demons and the television coverage was only possible thanks to special contrast filters and computer processing.

When the judge entered the courtroom, everyone got up and Sophia interrupted her commentary, switching to live audio.

"The hearing is open," said Tom Salomon, flipping through the investigation file.

The public prosecutors Bernard Louis and Natalie Brinne were sitting in the front row and Nick Valance with detective Moroni and his secretary, Linda, sat a few metres away. The accused looked indifferent in the corner cell. Showing great decency, the previous evening the public prosecutor had sent a text message to the lawyer, wishing him a serene and fair confrontation, hoping that justice would prevail. Nick thanked him, but doubted that it was going to be serene.

The chancellor called everyone's attention: "Procedure number 666: the international community against Lucifer Satan, known as Beelzebub, the accused. Charge: having damned the world".

Strange coincidences had caused the number 666 to be recurrent in the documents.

The charges were listed: "Subversive associations aimed at usurping power, uprising and attack against the head of a kingdom, breaking and entering in Eden, moral plagiarism and exploiting vulnerability in men, smuggling of the fruits of knowledge, instigating people to commit crimes, contempt for religion, torture of the damned."

"How does the accused plead?" the judge asked the defence lawyer.

"Not guilty," Nick replied.

There was a surprised buzz of voices.

"Silence." Salomon warned, "We shall continue."

The deputy attorney Bernard Louis stood up, addressing the members of the jury. "Ladies and gentlemen, the accused needs no presentation. His reputation precedes him, from the heavens to the depths of hell, with radically different meanings. Nobody on Earth has any doubts about his responsibilities and his guilt, but human law requires proof. We will soon provide this proof." He approached the jury. "Your honour and members of the jury, the prosecution will demonstrate, with extreme ease, the prisoner's guilt, asking that the maximum sentence be inflicted upon him: the death penalty."

"Objection, your honour," the defence attorney challenged immediately. "This procedure cannot violate the international rules. The defence asks that, if the accused is found guilty, he be sentenced to imprisonment and be subjected to a rehabilitation programme for his social rehabilitation."

There was amazed murmuring in the room and a few members of the public whistled mockingly.

The judge took note replying, "This will be deferred to the jury. The plaintiff may speak now".

A fat man with a long black moustache got up with difficulty from his seat. The Spanish lawyer Gonzales had been a promising bullfighter before undertaking his legal career. "In the name of every religion, we ask for compensation for the evil elicited in the world by the accused. In the event of insolvency, Hell shall be repossessed."

"The defence shall respond," the judge ordered.

Nick Valance got up. "Your honour, ladies and gentlemen of the jury, during this trial, the defence will demonstrate not only that there is only circumstantial evidence against Mr Satan, but also that he has so far been the victim of a plot to damage him, a gigantic conspiracy designed in very high places almost above suspicion, and he will ask that the real culprit be tried in his place".

"And who would this real culprit be, Mr Valance?" the judge asked, looking perplexed.

"I cannot disclose this information at present, your honour."

"Then let us begin with the documentary evidence."

∽ ∽ ∽

The documentary evidence was essentially the Sacred Scriptures, indicated by the public prosecution as "Exhibit A". The Vedas and the Hindu Bhagavadgita, the Buddhist Tapitaka, the Zoroastrian Avesta, the Hebrew Talmud, the Christian New Testament, the Muslim Koran, the Book of Mormon and other texts lay inert on the table of the chancery, like implacable accusers.

Before an extremely competent public, Nick tried to cast doubt about their authenticity. "The Old and New Testaments represent "a covenant", an agreement that God made with the men of that period. However, the form used, the testament, is inappropriate, since a regular contract would be needed. Furthermore, both documents appear to be lacking a signature: both God and men neglected to sign them, and therefore these documents are null and void."

The public prosecutor's eyes widened.

"These agreements," Nick continued "were imposed upon men without their consent, with evident violation of the freedom to negotiate, and they contain a good ten commandments, or unfair contract terms, that have turned out to be illegitimate."

"Your honour," Bernard Louis proclaimed, "God's two Testaments are all that legal culture of that time could produce."

"Even God?" the lawyer said sarcastically.

The judge scratched his head. Considering the irrelevance of the issue, he ordered, "The objection made by the prosecution is sustained. Please continue".

Nick did not desist. "In any case, the Devil's guilt is endorsed only by these texts". He raised the Bible in the air, showing it to the courtroom and to the television cameras. "And philological analyses have demonstrated numerous interpolations in the originals over the centuries. Even if it is the word of God, these are still human manipulations."

"This is irrelevant, your honour," the magistrate insisted once more. "The content of the texts is nevertheless valid."

"Uhm, sustained," the judge decreed again.

Nick took the blow, but continued all the same, "In the book of *Genesis*, it says that God created the sun four days after creating the light... and this is because, based on ancient beliefs, light existed independently of the sun. Although inspired by God, the author does not go beyond the limits of knowledge at that time".

Bernard did not let this trouble him. "God wanted to instil the truth without interfering in human culture, in order to respect our freedom".

"God could have raised men to his level, but he preferred to lower himself to theirs. It shall be put on record that God did not instil any culture into men."

A sense of perplexity pervaded the public and nobody really understood the lawyer's conclusion. Even when he moved to the analysis of the New Testament, the defence's goal appeared obscure.

"Why should we trust in the authenticity of the canonical Gospels?" Nick asked. "Before the Church formed the "Canon" in the Fourth century, multiple versions of the Gospels existed and were in circulation authoritatively throughout the empire: *the Gospel of Philip, the Protoevangelium of James, the Gospel of Thomas* and others that the Church only rejected as apocryphal later on. The criterion on which this choice was based, constructing the impenetrable bastions of orthodoxy, is still a mystery."

"The Holy Spirit illuminated the Church in the choice of those that were authentic," Bernard replied quite simply.

"But the Church was built on Christ's mandate, conferred through the gospels, which were not written by Christ but by the founders of the Church itself. It is a mandate of dubious legitimacy!"

The public prosecutor hesitated, while a soft buzz of voices encouraged him, and he consulted with his colleague, Brinne, before replying: "The Holy Spirit gave the apostles a complete knowledge of their master's life and they were thus able to talk about it in full".

"And how can the contradictions between the Gospels be justified? The different genealogies attributed to Jesus? The different descriptions of his life? The so-called "synoptic" question?

Louis turned to the judge, "Your honour, are we here to try God or the Devil? The defence is trying to shift the focus! We cannot doubt the documentary evidence because we would end up doubting everything".

The judge looked at Valance, waiting for him to answer.

"Your honour, I am merely trying to reconstruct the facts," Nick asserted.

"The facts are those that will prevail at the end of the trial," the judge ruled, "and there are no truths outside of the trial. The prosecution's observation is allowed. The hearing shall refer to witness evidence."

Lively enthusiasm followed the end of the hearing and Valance returned to his seat, where Frank and Linda were sitting in silence.

An overjoyed Bernard Louis joined him, his robes waving around his robust body. "You disappoint me a little, Mr Valance. Doubting the authenticity of a text means fearing a confrontation with its content. I thought you were more daring than that."

Nick did not seem worried: "Yet the prosecution's only witnesses are dead people, the identity of whom has never been legally confirmed, and they were often personally involved in the facts. Do you think you can demonstrate their word during this trial?"

Louis shrugged.

"In any case," the lawyer concluded, "I will try not to disappoint you again during the next hearings."

∽ ∽ ∽

Sophia Madlane entered the Rathaus building, the Zurich town hall, after being frisked by the guards. The journalist had been waiting for days to speak to the people who had organized and pushed for the trial, so that she could get an understanding of the interests involved.

In the baroque building on the Limmat river, the highest-ranking state officials had come together in a top-level meeting.

"I have an appointment with President Renard, for an interview," Sophia said to the security staff.

"I fear that it will not be possible today," they told her, "the president is going to be busy until this evening."

"But the appointment was made days ago!"

"The President is not receiving anyone today."

At that moment, Renard came down the stairs with the Swiss President and a group of assistants.

The woman took the opportunity to greet him and approach him. "Mr President, I'm Sophia Madlane of the *New York Times*. We have an appointment for an interview".

"I'm sorry, my dear, but as you can see I'm busy today," the French President replied smiling broadly. "My secretary will make another appointment for you for next week."

"You're avoiding me, Mr President!"

61

"Oh no, the Devil is a constant emergency, Miss, and anyway, I don't think I would have much to say to your readers on the other side of the ocean."

"No, my readers would be interested in knowing about the way you are handling this event."

"Nothing transcendent, we're just doing our best."

"You are preventing scientists and biologists from studying the accused and treating him like a circus freak!"

"Oh, is this what you want to talk about? Not today." The president waved at the security services to move the woman away and he headed towards the council chamber where other heads of state awaited him, away from the journalists.

Sophia stayed in the entrance hall, frustrated and powerless.

A few metres away, the German chancellor was standing in front of the window, contemplating the streets with their skeletal, icy trees, that had mysteriously withered throughout the city, under a leaden sky filled with dark omens. Catching Sophia's eye, he lifted his glass.

"The world has stopped turning," he said to her, "as if it were awaiting the outcome of the trial, so that it can reawaken…"

6

Witnesses for the prosecution

You shall not fall in with the many to do evil, nor shall you bear witness in a lawsuit, siding with the many, so as to pervert justice. Nor shall you be partial to a poor man in his lawsuit.

Exodus 23:2 et seq.

The roads of the major cities were all deserted. Only a few stray dogs roamed around, digging through the rubbish, unaware of what was going on in the world. Humanity had screeched to a halt, hypnotised in front of the television for the new episode of the most fascinating series ever produced. "The greatest television show of the last few centuries" - as the production company had playfully defined it - had been a big success with public and critics right from the beginning.

In the main courtroom of the Gerichtsgebäude, everything was ready for the important hearing, with the first witness for the prosecution, the demon informer who had made it possible to capture Satan. The people had been awaiting this event, positioning themselves around the Palace of Justice. When an armoured car escorted by numerous squad cars stopped in front of the entrance, armed men quickly jumped out and accompanied the strange being into the building. The audience at home watched with bated breath, as the television cameras followed the scene, capturing fragmented images: the witness walked along the corridor, entered the courtroom surrounded by policemen, sat at a bench before the judge and scratched his horns.

The attorney, Louis, cleared his throat. "Would you tell us your name, please?"

"I have been called witness Zeta" said the demon, with an electronically disguised voice, while his video image looked grainy.

"Do you come from a place called Hell?"

"It's difficult for you to understand, but I live in *Enfer*, an antithetical world located beneath the surface of the Earth."

"Were you once an angel? Did you rebel against the Creator? Please tell us about the famous revolt."

"I was an angel," he confirmed, "and I was involved in the revolt because I believed in several promises… but it was a huge misunderstanding."

"Do you know the accused here present?" Louis asked, pointing at Satan in his cell. The witness could see him through a one-way mirror panel, but Satan could not see him.

"He is the leader of the *Enfer*," the witness replied.

"Do you know God as well?"

"God? … The name of the Supreme One is taboo down there," the demon continued with a slight hesitation, "Nobody dares pronounce his name in vain but, for some of us, that name still holds a certain charm. Many feel nostalgia for the clouds, where the air is fresh and rarefied, but they do not admit it, for fear of the consequences."

"Yet you were able to do so: you escaped from Hell and have converted."

"I felt that what I was doing was wrong… that it was not right to work for a world without light. Therefore, I let myself be captured willingly, to expiate my sins and help men to build a new kingdom."

The audience looked in wonder, as they heard about such an unprecedented gesture. The demon had agreed with the magistrates about the version to give in the courtroom.

"This is proof that anyone can obtain salvation," Bernard concluded. "Redemption has a retroactive effect," he said, and then turned to address the judge. "Your honour, in view of this repudiation, the public prosecution requests the rehabilitation of the witness".

There was a timid round of approving applause from the audience, which was almost immediately suffocated by the lawyer, Mr Valance, who got up as he flipped through the report made by the Paris police.

"You were surprised while committing an offence in the French underground railway, as you tried to molest a female passenger," he said to the demon. "Was that part of your duties or was it the result of your conversion?"

A low rumble in the audience turned into embarrassment. The television cameras focused first on the lawyer and then on the witness, who confessed, "I had never been to Earth... I wanted to try out the sensations of your world".

"That's irrelevant, your honour," Louis hurriedly replied. "The witness has provided an essential contribution to capturing the accused. Even though he gave in to some instincts, we must keep his very nature in mind."

The judge agreed. «Mr Valance, do you wish to question the witness any further?"

Nick nodded. Satan had suggested the informer's probable name to him. In the silence of the courtroom, he scrutinized the demon: "Your name in code is Zeta... like Zepar, is that not so? Zepar is a demon who disappeared from Hell months ago never to return".

The demon, turning pale, looked at the prosecution bench, perplexed. "What if it were true?"

Valance replied: "How much did they pay you, Mr Zepar, to repudiate and betray your boss? More or less than thirty pieces of silver?"

The judge's eyes widened. Zepar looked around, confused.

"Answer the question!" Nick urged. "Did they open an account for you in some tax haven?"

"But that's not why I did it..."

"I have no further questions, your honour" Nick concluded, going back to his seat.

Feeling the unrest in the audience, the judge decided to suspend the hearing.

"The reference to thirty pieces of silver and the betrayal by Judas Iscariot was audacious and alarming," Pope Teomondo III complained on television. "The defence is confusing the sacred with the profane."

"Despite the great emotional impact" the journalist Sophia Madlane concluded, "the informer's testimony did not prove to be decisive for the trial, as it did not amount to any specific crime committed by Satan. The little demon was unaware of his boss's activities."

As the super-witness left the courtroom, the journalists crowded around with microphones and television cameras, but the demon was led into an armoured car and escorted to the airport. There was a Jesuit in the car, whose task was to educate him properly in the doctrine of the faith. The young demon was to be put on a military aeroplane and sent to an unknown destination.

Nobody would ever hear of him again.

∞ ∞ ∞

The next day, the trial continued with the interrogation of other witnesses. In his pure white robes, Teomondo III was next on the witness stand. The TV producer complained because such whiteness created a halo effect on the video. The College of Cardinals had disapproved of his decision, stating, "Any testimony against the Devil is unthinkable and a confrontation between the Holy Father and such a creature is degrading". Nevertheless, Teomondo was adamant: he absolutely wanted to play an active role in the event and the Catholic audience enthusiastically welcomed the first legal testimony by a head of the Church.

Bernard Louis, who had agreed upon the content of the interrogation with the Pope, began, "Would you tell us your full name, please?"

"The name I adopted when I was elected Pope is Teomondo III."

"As the successor of St Peter, can you tell the jury whether or not the Devil has always been a constant presence in the history of mankind and if it is he who leads man into temptation and is responsible for the tragedies of our history?"

"The Devil stays away from all that is sacred," the Pope asserted, "just like darkness will shy away from the light, though everyone can feel his presence in the world. Where there is immorality, dissoluteness and depravation, there is also evil."

"Has he caused a great deal of damage, based on your experience?"

"A huge amount, both moral and material. This is why ministers of consolation and exorcists exist and fight him."

"In canon law, are there any extenuating circumstances for his crimes?"

"His punishment is an essential part of the divine plan."

"Thank you," the magistrate said, looking satisfied.

Immediately afterwards, the lawyer, Valance, got up for the cross-examination and, approaching the figure dressed in white, he asked, "You do not frequent immoral environments, is that true Mr Teomondo?"

"Of course not."

"Therefore, you have never seen the Devil at work and hence you cannot testify to any calamity provoked by him."

«No, but I know the impact of his work."

"Nevertheless the Church has never put the existence of the Devil nor his evil among the dogmas of religion. Let the record show that the witness has not seen the accused commit any crime."

"One moment," the Pope said, getting up. "A few days ago this foul being injured the eye of my assistant, father Cimor!"

The crowd became restless. Upright and surrounded by an air of integrity, Teomondo stood out like the pillar of a Cathedral.

"Silence!" the judge ordered. "The witness shall limit himself to answering the questions using respectful language."

"I have no further questions, your honour," Valance concluded.

When the hearing came to an end, to the relief of all, the Pope was filmed as he walked away, escorted by the Swiss guards, until he disappeared in a halo of light along the corridor.

Between one advert and another, men of religion and mystics from every religion and from all over the world sat and testified in the trial - a variety of doctrines against a common enemy.

"The Devil alters human behaviour by hindering judgement of the new truths," a protestant reverend declared.

A Hindu Brahman added, "The spirit of evil has a thousand faces and a thousand images: it reincarnates in creatures and hides in earthly matter".

It was then Rabbi Tariz's turn. He wore his traditional black robes, with a *kippa*, a skullcap, on his head. "The Talmud, our doctrine, is clear on this subject: evil needs to be punished".

"But if I am not mistaken, in the New Testament, God told man that he must not judge," Nick suggested.

"Oh no, it was not God who said that, but Jesus… and Jesus was one of the many prophets at that time. The Torah, however, which is the heart of Judaism, was written by God himself, on Mount Sinai."

Disapproving mumbling could be heard and the plaintiff's lawyer got up. "Your honour, the fact that Jesus and God are *consubstantial,* that they are of the same substance, is a dogma".

"The Christian Trinity is in contrast with Biblical teachings," the rabbi insisted, "and the Bible is *our* text. Nobody can be the son of himself."

There was considerable disapproval in the docks, pushing the Pope to intervene, "After thousands of years, you are awaiting the messiah in vain: it was Jesus".

"Jesus could not have been Allah!" said the Muslim imam, as a microphone hovered over the audience. "Jesus was a new man, like Adam, but he was not crucified: his death was an illusion created for the people. The Koran is explicit: you need to welcome Mohammed, the last great prophet and the seal of all the Words."

The disapproval extended to the other creeds.

The Hindu Brahman challenged, "Western religions venerate the resurrection of the body, as if the body were the most important thing, but they ignore the reincarnation of the soul".

"Here we go," Bernard Louis murmured, foreseeing what was about to happen.

"You don't have to believe in God to believe in reincarnation," a Buddhist bonze commented.

"Buddhism reveals a creeping atheism," the other replied. "The Gods exist and the Christian Trinity comes from our *Trimurti*: the trinity of Brahma, Shiva and Vishnu."

"However, the Holy Spirit continues on *through* the Father and the Son and not *from* the Father and the Son," the orthodox patriarch pointed out, entering into controversy with the Catholics.

The television cameras moved quickly over the faces of the religious leaders, confused by ancient disputes that had been revived in the courtroom.

"The wisest one was Lao Tse!" said a Taoist master. "He was conceived as a sunbeam and generated from the left armpit of a virgin after a pregnancy that lasted 80 years!"

He was immediately drowned out by whistling.

As the theological confrontation degenerated, the clerks intervened to bring order back to the courtroom.

"Ladies and gentlemen, we are in court, not in church!" the judge shouted. "And as for you, Mr Valance, I forbid you to stir up any other similar discord."

"Your honour, I was merely interrogating the witness," said Nick, defending himself.

It was Louis, the public prosecutor, who calmed everyone down: "Ladies and gentlemen, the differences between the various religions must not make us lose sight of our common goal: our aversion to evil. Therefore, instead of wasting our energy, let's concentrate on Beelzebub".

"The trial is adjourned" the judge decreed.

∽∽∽

The television and subsequent debates dedicated ample space to what went on during the hearing, shedding light on the contradictions between the religions and hoping for greater coordination between the various creeds. Keeping this in mind, Teomondo III carried out a series of consultations between the Christian leaders, but the space for dialogue was limited. The Orthodox Church had been separated from the Catholic Church with the East–West Schism of 1054, from the Protestant Church by the Lutheran Reform of 1517, becoming fragmented into numerous other Churches, hard to place under a single roof. All these Churches, all these *lost shepherds*, had different sacraments and different liturgies; and they did not recognize each other's authority.

When the trial resumed, the exorcist, father Cimor, declared that he was willing to give his contribution to the truth. The incident inflicted upon him by his rival had made him more famous, turning him into a living martyr.

Before the television cameras, he was accompanied to the stand, where his figure, dressed in his black robes, appeared even more gaunt. A glass eye, the result of the incident with the Devil, now glistened in his face.

"I have met the Devil during my work as an exorcist," he said into the microphone. "I have fought him to free the souls and the bodies that he possessed." He glanced at his enemy in the cage, who was listening unperturbed, as the sky became dark and a droning noise could be heard coming from outside. "I have seen possessed women speak in Aramaic, rotating their heads unnaturally, walking backwards down the stairs, uttering all kinds of profanities."

"What were the effects of all this?"

"The spreading of sins, immorality, libertinism, the persecution of religious people…" Faint and subdued, the droning sound was like the wind whispering through the leaves, but it soon became more persistent.

"His work, Satan's hand, was always behind all of that."

One spectator got up, pointing to the side windows, and the television cameras followed, confused: a dense greyish cloud was obscuring the view. The television cameras zoomed in, revealing the cause of the phenomenon.

"Flies!" someone yelled.

A thick swarm of flies had gathered outside the courtroom windows: thousands, millions of flies, had surrounded the Palace of Justice, wrapping it in a gloomy embrace.

Among the worshippers surrounding the building, there was a disorderly stampede and incidents were taking place. A helicopter took off to try to break up the siege and several journalists were able to capture the scene: the entire tribunal was hidden by a cloud of bugs.

Although the building's entrances were locked, numerous insects managed to get inside, making the public panic. Judge Salomon looked around, confused. Bernard Louis hurriedly stuffed the documents into his briefcase. Frank Moroni, who was next to Mr Valance, took out his 38 calibre and Cimor recited verses in Latin, while the Satanist Yorgo Mirakis raised his arms to the sky.

The firemen used flamethrowers to stop the attack, large fires began to blaze in front of the entrances and slowly prevailed over the flies.

It was the journalist Sophia Madlane who restored the broadcast at the Palace of Justice after the disconcerting phenomenon. The cloud of insects had been replaced by a rain cloud that brought a heavy shower.

The television image showed the woman's face, with her wet hair over her shoulders: "A unique occurrence took place during today's hearing: a swarm of flies invaded the Palace of Justice and fear filled the air for several minutes among those present. It was feared that this was an apocalyptic sign. Then, as quickly and mysteriously as they had arrived, the flies disappeared. Several entomologists were consulted, to find a scientific explanation for the phenomenon, but someone suspected that it had been caused by the supernatural intervention of Beelzebub, the Lord of the flies.

While the court was cleared and careful pest control measures were being carried out on the premises, a few flies remained in the corridors and on the ceiling of the main courtroom. One of the flies approached the accused's cell and buzzed around it for a while before landing on the glass and entering the cell through a ventilation hole. Satan smiled, seeing the insect land on the palm of his hand: it was a messenger from the kingdom of darkness and it had come to tell him that his demons were nearby.

7

The Devil's ways

> Blessed are those who are persecuted for righteousness' sake.

> *Gospel according to Matthew* 5:10

The steel door opened noisily in front of Yorgo Mirakis, the Satanist, who entered the prison visiting room, accompanied by two guards. The lost angel, the rebel of the skies, was sitting before him behind a glass panel, chained up and waiting in silence. Ever since the moment of his capture, Yorgo had wanted to meet his spiritual master in person and had tirelessly continued to ask for a meeting with him, until after various requests, the lawyer, Mr Valance, had succeeded in getting him permission.

In the visiting room, which was normally crammed full of prisoners' friends and relatives, but was now empty, the Satanist approached his idol, filled with nervous excitement.

"'Hail, O Satan, O rebellion, O you avenging force of human reason!'" he recited, quoting Giosuè Carducci. "I am Yorgo Mirakis, representative of your sects, the Church of Satan, the Fraternitas Saturni and the Temple of Set. I have always tried to be in contact with the Underworld…"

"I cannot bear flatterers," the Devil answered.

"Please forgive me...," the clergyman apologised. "I am here to offer you my services and those of your confraternities."

The devil pulled out a bunch of admiring letters sent by Satanists and pushed them through the communication window: "Give them back to the senders. I do not intend to read them. I do not want disciples who always remain so. I do not speak to populations, I do not speak to Churches. Just like religions, your sects do not contribute in any way to man's independence. Furthermore," he concluded, "I have no use for your devotion".

"But... prince," Yorgo was visibly confused and gulped several times, "I thought you liked being venerated."

"I am not a model created in God's image," Satan replied. "I only accepted this talk so that I could clarify the things that should already have been clear. If you want my will to be done, forget me. Only when you no longer need me, when you live without invisible means of support, when you have lost me... only then will my will have been done."

Beads of sweat formed on Yorgo's forehead; he had dedicated his life to the worship of Satan and now his words felt like the lashes of a whip. "We will change," he promised, "we will perfect your doctrine based on your wishes."

"Only a fool would entrust the preaching of his own doctrine to others."

"So what must we do?"

The prince of darkness pondered for a moment and then a vague spark seemed to flicker in his eyes.

"Maybe you could do something..."

"I will do anything," Yorgo grunted, with a hint of hope in his voice.

Satan spoke slowly, in a barely understandable Greek dialect, "*Epicalumai enon diabolon*... evoke a devil, in my name. Are you capable of doing this, to get a message to him?"

"Evoking devils is my job," Yorgo assured him.

The guards and the television cameras were far enough away for the prince of darkness to scratch a word on the glass, using the tip of his fingernail, writing it backwards so that Yorgo could read it. It was a word of a few letters in a foreign language:

TETRAGRAMMATON.

Yorgo frowned, straining to memorize it.

"You must communicate with the Underworld, with Astaroth or with Asmodeus," Satan said, "because I need to see Bensoria, the only one who can offer me his help."

"Astaroth, Asmodeus, Bensoria...," Yorgo nodded several times and then got up and called the guards, asking them to let him out.

The prisoner scratched the glass to obscure the word and, when the officers came to get him, a spark had returned to light up his eyes. The fire inside him was still burning.

∽ ∽ ∽

A procession of worshippers filled the city streets. Sacred hymns and psalms rang out from the procession, along with incense, rising up towards the sky. The strange atmosphere of those days was reawakening religious vocations all over the world and numerous millenarian sects that referred to the book of *Revelation* and were convinced that Christ would return at the end of the trial to imprison Satan and reign for a thousand years.

The dull winter sun reflected on the Palace of Justice, lighting up the Swiss city. After the fly incident, the trial had resumed and more precautions had been taken: the windows had been equipped with mosquito blinds and the guards were wearing special protective helmets. The number of members of public present had decreased, but the television audience had increased and the prosecution was feeling quite satisfied.

The hearing had not yet started, when a group of men entered the courtroom and headed towards the judge's bench. The television cameras followed their movements, while policemen tried to hold them back.

"Let me speak to the judge!" said the man leading the group, breaking away and reaching the judge's bench. "Judge, stop this farce, this grotesque scheme triggered by the governments!"

"Who are you?" Salomon asked, motioning the guards to stop.

«I'm a scientist! I'm here to express my indignation. Why waste time with this farce, when we could be studying this creature instead? Why not try to understand his role in the evolution of our species?"

Heated comments were circulating through the public. Scientists have always fought to spread the rationalist method and this trial was an insult to them.

"The existence of metaphysics is a scientific paradox," he said, "and wasting resources to try this being is senseless! If man comes from the monkey, and not from God, continuing along this path makes no sense."

"But this is not a scientific meeting," the judge explained, "and we are not applying the laws of nature here, but human laws."

"The Devil is the people's portrayal of all our fears, a scapegoat for humanity! It is easier to hate the Devil than to love man. This trial is an alibi for our guilty consciences!"

The judge looked like he was reflecting, before pronouncing himself. "Considering the physical evidence of the accused, the objection is overruled."

Concluding the issue, he had the guards accompany the scientists outside.

In the meeting held later on in his studio, in which the Satanist Mirakis also participated, the lawyer, Mr Valance, had to acknowledge the fact that the line of defence he had followed so far had failed.

In the presence of his assistants, he carefully analysed the situation, recognizing that the accusations were still solid.

"If opposing the prosecution's legitimacy has proved to be useful," he said, "we now need to oppose its merit."

"Its merit?" the others replied, giving him questioning looks.

"We must admit the facts," he explained. "But we need a theology expert capable of interpreting them."

Yorgo Mirakis hesitated, "Mr Valance, I don't know if our sects have enough money to fund all of this".

"Defending the Devil requires a great deal of investment. We have centuries of theology to examine."

Yorgo touched the scar on his cheek.

"During the next hearings" the lawyer concluded "we will have to play our trump card."

∽ ∽ ∽

A shining moon tore through the veil of clouds and shed its light on a villa on the Zurichberg, the wooded hill north of Zurich. In a lounge lit up by black candles, Yorgo Mirakis, wrapped in a black habit, raised his goblet and addressed the hooded men present: "It is midnight, brothers. Draw the pentagram".

He had not revealed the content of his conversation with the prisoner to the lawyer and had kept this important mission to himself. It was now time to bring it to fulfilment.

In front of the little flames flickering along the walls, his assistants drew the symbol on the floor, with the blood of an animal, chanting as they went.

Deep in concentration, Yorgo expressed the magic formula three times: "*Tetragrammaton, Tetragrammaton, Tetragrammaton*" and then fell into a trance.

With a quiver, his body stiffened and his pupils turned white; the worshippers said nothing, as an unnatural silence filled the place.

A gust of wind made the windows in the building vibrate and blew out the candles. In the darkness, something icy caressed the backs of the men's necks, as a greenish vapour seemed to be materializing within the pentagram. Scared and incredulous, they stood watching the phenomenon.

A rattling noise was heard, coming from another dimension, as a figure slowly took shape. The demon that appeared had the face of a male goat, with curved horns and grey down, but the image was distorted by the transmission and he was probably worse in real life.

"Who evokes me?"

Yorgo declared, "I am Mirakis, the priest. I need to communicate with the devil Asmodeus or the devil Astaroth".

The image in the centre of the pentagram muttered: "I am Azazel, the demon of the desert. You have made a mistake!" He then vanished, mumbling, leaving a mound of sand on the floor.

With some difficulty, Mirakis came out of the trance and dried his forehead before checking the formula, feeling confused. "Yet, this is it..." He concentrated again, trying to pronounce it more precisely: "*Te-tra-gram-ma-ton*".

This time, after a gust of wind, a colourful vapour appeared.

"I would like to speak with Asmodeus or Astaroth...," the priest said again. "I have a message from Satan."

«From Satan?» a female voice replied. "Wait."

Some background noise could be heard and then the candles lit themselves again, flaring up, and a male voice accompanied the materialization of a figure in the centre of the symbol.

"Asmodeus."

He was quite a captivating demon: blond, with curly hair and robust.

"I am Yorgo Mirakis… high priest of Satanism. I have an important message from Satan. He gave it to me personally at the prison in which he is being held."

"I'm listening," said the demon.

"Satan says that… well, he wants to see someone.. I can't remember the name exactly... Ah yes, a certain Bensoria. He says that only she can help him."

"Bensoria?" The word seemed to float around in the air. Touching the cleft on his chin, the demon meditated in silence. "Anything else?"

"This is all, I think" Yorgo confirmed. "I do not know who this woman is."

"Hell is grateful to you, man" he concluded.

The image in the centre of the pentagram disappeared leaving just the distant sound of whispering, "Sorry, my dear, I have to go…"

When Yorgo Mirakis woke up from his state of trance, tired and covered in sweat, he fell to the floor and his men came to prop him up. Although he was tired, he also felt proud: the message had been sent and now *they* would deal with it.

∽∽∽

Unaware of what had happened during the night, Nick Valance went to the maximum security prison of Horgen early in the morning and asked to speak to his client. After some difficulty, he was accompanied to Satan's cell.

The Devil was hanging from a corner of the ceiling like a large bat, with two big black wings wrapped around his body. The cable radio was transmitting the *Mephisto Walz* by Liszt in the background, a small concession provided by the prison warden.

"Mr Satan," he said into the microphone.

The Devil muttered something unclear before coming down from the ceiling. His bat wings retracted behind his shoulder blades, revealing a semi-naked body.

"Are you willing to testify?" the lawyer asked.

"Testify?"

"Tell your version of the facts at the trial."

"To what end?" the Devil asked, while his shadow continued to flutter with open wings on the wall. "Nobody takes you seriously when you are considered a slanderer."

"We must oppose the prosecution's case."

"There are no alibis for Hell."

"We will try to push a camel through the eye of a needle. It will be our *probatio diabolica*."

Satan thought about it, still sluggish: "And what should I say exactly?"

"The same things you told me."

"Everything?"

Nick nodded, with a faint smile.

The Devil grumbled in an unknown language, then leapt onto the ceiling and went back to his previous position, hanging upside down. With a swishing noise, his wings opened again and wrapped around him.

His answer was silence.

8

The broken sky

> How you are fallen from heaven, O Day Star, son of Dawn!

Isaiah 14:12

The news of the Devil's testimony spread quickly through the mass media, arousing both interest and unrest everywhere. The religious leaders were worried, fearing that his testimony might upset the worshippers' spiritual balance. The orthodox patriarch was pessimistic, "If God has denied the Devil the right to speak for thousands of years, there must be a reason. What might come out of that mouth?"

But public opinion was electrified and the religious communities in fibrillation. Despite there being no more rooms free in Zurich, pilgrims continued to meet in Switzerland, convinced that it was Armageddon, the place indicated by the prophecies for the final battle. Long traffic jams had formed along the city's main thoroughfares, packed with caravans and camper vans, and the UN forces intervened to set up a makeshift camp and emergency catering services.

The Devil's testimony went beyond a simple trial. It was a voice emerging from the depths of time, the echo of an unknown past: it was a story told by the only witness to the most important page of history.

The prosecution, however, was indifferent and did not consider the interrogation of the accused to be in any way risky and, instead, hoped that, in this way, his culpability would be defined more rapidly.

The Satanist, Mirakis, was interviewed on the subject.

"Has the Devil's version of the facts ever been listened to?" they asked him. "Do you believe that this will change the worship of Lucifer?"

«Satanism has never been an unveiled cult," he admitted. "With this testimony, the risk is that it will become more popular and less restricted to an *elite* than it is now; it will not be possible to damage it."

When the judge ordered, "The accused shall now be interrogated", everyone held their breath. It was the high point of the trial.

"This is the trial of his and our lives," the journalist Sophia Madlane commented, live from the courthouse. "The Devil has decided to bring his centuries-old actions into play, by accepting this questioning. Will he be capable of not lying?"

"We call upon Lucifer Satan, also known as Beelzebub, to testify."

The cage that had been guarding the accused creaked as it was opened, sounding like the lament of a tormented soul, and the Devil was led out and accompanied to the witness stand. As he passed, a gust of cold air lowered the temperature in the room. The television cameras got a close-up image of the Devil as he was chained to the chair; focusing on his deep-set eyes that caused dizziness.

"Swear… on Hell that you will tell the truth, the whole truth and nothing but the truth", the clerk of the court recited.

"I do not usually swear," the accused replied, while a light sulphurous vapour came out of the floor around him.

"The world will have to be wary of the things I say and those that I do not say."

The deputy attorney, Natalie Brinne, an expert on canon law, had asked to question him personally and so she approached him. As highlighted in the press, the fact that a woman was accusing him was extremely significant: in this way, the seduction of which Eve had been a victim at the beginning of time would be redeemed.

The television cameras focused on the woman's delicate face, her glasses and her short blond hair.

"Would you tell us your full name please?"

The accused smiled enigmatically. "I have many names, but man has always preferred to call me Satan." That word grated noisily in the microphone.

"But you are also known as Lucifer, Beelzebub, Iblis, Abaddon and Belial… is that right?" the woman urged.

"You can call me anything you like" he said, "but not Lucifer!" "Lucifer is the name of an angel that no longer exists."

She acknowledged his words. "Is it true, Mr Satan, that you rebelled against the Creator thousands of years ago, when you were an angel, thereby provoking a war?"

"It corresponds to the truth," he answered.

There was a murmuring among the audience.

"And is it true that you, having taken on the form of a serpent, allured the first human couple, Adam and Eve, in the Garden of Eden, and encouraged them to disobey God?"

"Yes."

"So it was your fault that Adam and Eve stole the sinful fruit from the forbidden tree, triggering the fury of God?"

He nodded.

"Your honour, the accused has confessed!" Brinne exclaimed. "And was it also you who tempted Jesus Christ in the desert and hindered the work of the prophets of every religion?"

"I tried to bring them back down to Earth."

"And is it also you, Mr Satan, who still tempts the worshippers today?"

"They often have no need to be tempted."

"Last question: do you regret your rebellion?"

"If coherence is a virtue, then regret is a defect."

"We can say that the accused is a habitual offender," Natalie concluded. "It shall be recorded in the minutes that Mr Satan has confessed to all of his crimes."

A liberating applause followed and all the people in the courtroom rose to their feet. The theologians were enthusiastic: the prophecy of the *Genesis*, according to which a woman would one day bruise the serpent's head had come true. "She shall bruise your head, and you shall bruise her heel"

The audience increased dramatically and, to the dismay of the publicity agencies, all the commentators predicted an imminent conclusion to the trial.

Seated at his bench, Nick listened unperturbed.

∽ ∽ ∽

With the ringing of a bell, the activities resumed and the public awaited the defence's cross-examination with curiosity. The lawyer got up, adjusting his toga over his nut-brown suit, and approached the accused.

Bernard Louis whispered maliciously to his colleague, "Do you want to bet he'll try to blame society?"

In the general silence, the lawyer cleared his throat. "Mr Satan, tell us about your origins. Was your childhood like that of all the other angels?"

The Devil looked uneasy. "I was different," he said. "I was the first angel and I was moulded from the fire; with me,

God had created something that he never wanted to repeat: he had granted me free will. From the very beginning, I displayed critical thinking and a desire for independence. I remember endless solitude."

"I knew it," Louis said dryly. "He had a difficult childhood."

"But why did God create you?" Valance asked. "Did he not know the future? Did he not know that you would rebel one day?"

Satan bowed his head: "The future is indomitable. I am the obvious result of an error of judgment".

The judge frowned, the public prosecutors looked at each other, perplexed, and the lawyer hid a smile, "Mr Satan, did you participate in the creation of world?"

"I participated, but had a secondary role."

"What was your task?"

"I was assigned the job of guarding the world."

"So, you were a sort of *demiurge*, an intermediary that, according to numerous ancient religions, interfered in God's original plan?"

He did not answer.

"What led to the break-up of your relationship?"

"It was man."

"Please explain."

The accused seemed to hesitate. "I found the human animal attractive... the most successful of all the species. The previous attempt, the monkey, had been a disappointment. For this reason, I suggested that God give man more freedom and make him more autonomous than the others".

"And what did God say?"

"He refused. He scorned the idea."

"Why?"

"I asked myself that question too... a father always aspires to the growth of his own children. Yahweh is the only father who does not want his children to become like himself."

"What do you mean?"

"He didn't want any rivals."

"So, why did he create the world and the living species?"

The audience sat holding its breath... that question was vitally important and the greatest existential questions were on the tip of the Devil's tongue. Staring at the religious leaders in the first few rows, Satan spoke. "Yahweh was omnipotent, eternal, perfect. But he was also alone, absolutely and infinitely alone. And without any elements of comparison, he was unable to feel as immense as he wanted to. He had created the angels, but they did not satisfy him. That's why he created the animal species, which were even weaker, so that he could feel the wide gap between them and himself and enjoy this feeling of superiority".

This revelation struck the public, as the audience sat speechless before their televisions screens, unable to make any comments.

"So, God created man to satisfy an infinite desire to feel like God?" the lawyer ventured.

«Objection, your honour,» Bernard Louis protested. "God created man out of love: in order to satisfy the desire to be a father."

Scratching his head, the judge called the lawyer. "What is this story about God? Did you suggest it to him?"

"The story is original, your honour," Nick assured him.

"Accusations like this cannot be made," he said, still looking undecided. "Alright, you may proceed, but make sure your client moderates his language."

"I will do my best."

"The prosecution's objection is overruled," Tom Salomon ordered. "The last statements will be retained."

There was a great deal of surprised mumbling and the voices followed each other throughout the courtroom like circling doves.

Satisfied, the lawyer continued, "What happened when you noticed the reason for the creation?"

"I was disheartened," Lucifer answered. "The image of Lord God became opaque... and when the angels were ordered to honour man, a man like this, I objected, knowing that action was needed. By casting this doubt among the inhabitants of Heaven, I opened up a breach in the stability of the kingdom and I organized an opposition front against Heaven."

"What was the purpose of this?"

"To overthrow the divine dictatorship and establish a government of angels. Yahweh was an omnipotent monopolist and we could no longer accept this. We wanted to replace God's kingdom with a republic of angels."

"What?" the public prosecutor exclaimed.

Those present were lost in amazement.

"Therefore, the purpose of your resistance was democratic?" the lawyer suggested.

Satan took a deep breath: "War broke out. It was the War of the Heavens, and it was a war that shook the foundations of the world. Our ranks fought bravely, but God was invincible... With the angel Michael, he broke through our front lines and brutally suppressed the revolt. His thunderbolts ripped through the sky and many perished in the clouds, while others were taken captive. I was pierced by a bolt of lightning that burnt my heart, turning it to ashes".

As if evoked by the Devil, a sound of thunder and lightning echoed in the courtroom and the distant cries of angels could be heard clearly.

"Impromptu special effects!" the producer said with a jump.

The book of *Psalms* was broadcast on television as on-screen text:

> *The LORD also thundered in the heavens, and the Most High uttered his voice, hailstones and coals of fire, And he sent out his arrows and scattered them; he flashed forth lightnings and routed them. Then the channels of the sea were seen, and the foundations of the world were laid bare at your rebuke.*

The Devil suffocated his pain. The wounds in his chest and in his pride were still open.

"After the revolt had been tamed," he concluded, "Yahweh decided us to imprison us in the depths of the Earth. He made us material beings and let us fall."

"Why did he not kill you? Was it for divine mercy?" Valance asked.

"To remind himself of his triumph. It was a way of feeling even greater."

"Objection your honour!" Bernard reacted. "The accused is expressing personal opinions."

"Upheld," the judge ruled.

"Very well," Valance recognized, "but the Geneva Convention dictates respect for prisoners of war; why is this principle absent in Heaven?" He turned to the accused and said, "Will you show the world your true appearance?"

His chains were loosened. Lucifer got up, widening his shoulders and, to the audience's amazement, two large dark wings appeared behind him, tearing through his suit.

There was grumbling in the audience.

"Yahweh acted cruelly with our bodies," he said.

He moved the lock of hair from his forehead and showed his horns, then he unbuttoned his trousers and, despite the indignation of those present, pulled out a black tail.

"Put your clothes back on!" the judge ordered. "And as for you, Mr Valance, be careful, or you will be reported for obscene acts!"

The lawyer agreed respectfully but went on to specify, "The reason for all this is easy to see: God deformed his enemy to make him look evil and to ensure that man would not listen to him. He aimed at his physical form to avoid a direct confrontation about the content".

Public prosecutor Louis's jaw contracted, as the statement was directed at him.

∽ ∽ ∽

Broadcasting a panning shot of the room, the producer was as excited as a child: "No publicity, carry on filming!"

Nick paced theatrically before the accused, with his hands behind his back. The spectators followed him with bated breath. Bernard Louis scratched his jaw. The judge mopped his brow.

After the jury had digested the content of the statements, the lawyer continued his interrogation: "Tell us about Adam and Eve. Why did you tempt them?"

The memory of the angel reminded him of those distant events.

"I tried to free them." he answered. "God had confined them to the Garden of Eden so that they would cultivate it and guard it". But I had other plans for them: they could win the war that I had lost... I took on the appearance of a serpent, the most cunning of animals, and I slithered into Eden. In the middle of the Garden, next to the tree of life, stood the tree of knowledge. I approached Eve and revealed to her that, by eating the fruit of that tree, she would become free and autonomous like God. It was not a lie. With the knowledge of good and evil, man would discover moral evolution and would start to grow, to ascend and begin to lead his own life. Therefore Eve picked the fruit and ate some of it. She then offered it to Adam who, because of his love for her, did the same."

"So, Adam sinned to please Eve?" Valance interrupted. "Could it be said that man's original sin, as well as being a sin of gluttony, was also a sin of love?"

A little smile appeared on the face of the accused. "Curiosity also played an important role. Adam and Eve were like children. They were not ashamed of their nakedness and wanted to know about the world. I allowed them to become adults".

"Childhood, our lost paradise…," the lawyer commented.

Taking advantage of the situation, the television transmitted some on-screen text displaying a few verses of *Genesis*, with the serpent's words:

> *"For God knows that when you eat of it your eyes will be opened, and you will be like God, knowing good and evil." The tree was good for food, a delight to the eyes and to be desired to make one wise.*

"What happened after that?" Valance continued.

"As soon as they tasted the forbidden fruit, their eyes were opened and the two of them became aware of their condition: they saw that they were naked and felt ashamed. God had created them naked, like animals, prisoners of the physical body, because that is what he considered them. But with my help those puppets cut the strings that linked them to the puppet master and began to walk on their own. It was the greatest miracle that history has ever witnessed."

The word *miracle* left the spectators astounded. Lucifer shut his eyes tightly as he remembered that distant victory, and then carried on.

"Nevertheless the outcome did not last long. Awoken from his sleep, the Almighty come down to take a walk in the Garden, where he noticed something unusual in the humans' behaviour and realised that they had touched the fruit. He was furious, like only a god can be, and became aware that creating man had been a mistake. He had created a rival. Knowledge makes you similar to God: if man becomes scientific, it's the end for Yahweh."

The audience was silent.

"However, as science and culture can only prosper in conditions of well-being, it was necessary to prevent man from being too happy. For this reason, God exiled the two progenitors from Eden, forcing them to work for a living and to give birth with pain: work would weaken their limbs and pain would tame their spirit. So diseases, old age and death spread everywhere: these were all expedients to induce humans not to think and not to know, all strategies to hinder human growth... all tools for fighting science!"

The judge was dumbfounded. Marduk, the attorney general, who was watching from the screen in his office, was so thunderstruck that his pipe slipped out of his mouth.

The television channel was once again quick to broadcast the biblical verses:

> *Becoming aware of good and evil, man thus became like one of us. Now, lest he reach out his hand and take also of the tree of life and eat, and live forever.*

"So, that fruit didn't go down well with the whole of humanity!" Valance stated, pacing back and forth in front of the jury boxes. "But why was the Almighty unable to make himself heard?"

The accuser's voice quivered and the images returned to focus on his face. "Not content, after the first exodus, the first deportation in history, God wanted Adam and Eve to reproduce sexually, so that the original sin would perpetuate through the generations to come and torture them for eternity".

The audience shuddered, incredulous, and someone in the gallery fainted. Valance insinuated, "So God created sex so that he wouldn't have to get his hands dirty?"

"Mr Valance!" the judge reprimanded him.

"Yes, your honour… just one last question. But if God didn't want man to eat the apple, why did he leave the tree in the Garden of Eden? Could he not have moved it elsewhere?"

"In fact, he intended to move it," Lucifer confirmed, "but after creating the world, he was tired. I outguessed him at the weekend."

"The Devil, the idleness of God on the seventh day," Nick pointed out and then added, "So you took advantage of the fact that the Creator was distracted, to damn humanity for its own good?"

"I freed humanity from its original slavery. Through me, a journey was undertaken, the aim of which was to take man far away: thus progress began."

Bernard Louis got up and rushed forward. "Objection! History is being interpreted arbitrarily. And history tells us that, through tricks and deceit, the Devil persuaded humanity to violate the orders it had received: to alter man's blissful *status* by tasting an indigestible mouthful of knowledge, making life onerous and unhappy, with tragic consequences! Before that, all animals were living in harmony; but after the sin, the beasts became wild and, by imitating them, man became violent. When man lost Eden, he also lost the tree of life that grew there: he lost immortality! Death and corruptibility spread everywhere, infecting other species".

"The days of anger" Lucifer agreed, not in the least affected by the magistrate's ardour. "The whole of creation paid for the sin committed by a single man. Like a disillusioned artist who destroys his own work, the Almighty acted cruelly with the world. Angered with us devils for our unwanted participation, he relegated us to living beneath the land of mortals. Meanwhile, he wanted to see if man had redeemed himself or if he had continued to be disobedient…"

"Your honour" Louis insisted, "the interpretation of the episode according to canon law is different. The public prosecution requests that an expert be appointed to ascertain the truth!"

"An expert? Uhm… yes, that might be a good idea."

Speaking over the voices of those present, the judge ordered the immediate acquisition of evidence before suspending the hearing, with a sigh of relief. In the midst of the collective agitation, the Devil was taken back to his cell, overwhelmed by flashes from the cameras. He had an ineffable smile on his face. Discord had been planted.

∽ ∽ ∽

"Damn!" the attorney general, Marduk, exclaimed, banging his fists on the table in his private studio in the Gerichtsgebäude, his silver hair looking whiter than usual. "What's this story about the democratic uprising and the beginning of progress?"

The two public prosecutors shrugged.

"I'm sorry sir, but we couldn't have predicted a version like this one," Louis admitted. "We were caught unprepared."

"But the world is watching us!" Marduk roared. "Everyone wants an exemplary verdict. It shouldn't be difficult when you're up against the Devil… Every public prosecutor dreams about accusing the Devil!"

"I'm mortified, sir. We had underestimated the defence lawyer's ability."

"We must think about public opinion... Do you think it will be possible to contradict the version given by the accused?"

"Lucifer's version reflects the Biblical version," Natalie Brinne intervened. "Unfortunately, the Old Testament does not offer any interpretations of those facts…"

"I wouldn't dramatize too much, sir," Bernard reassured him. The doctrine of original sin was only theorized by St Augustine. The other religions have always ignored it and not even the Jews thought it was very important. We have other arguments for incriminating Satan, and other strings to our bow."

"Well, use them then!"

The telephone rang loudly.

"Hello, Mr President," the attorney general replied, loosening the knot in his tie. "It was impossible to foresee a similar version… it was an accident... Reassure the other governments... the situation is under control."

That evening, the slow movement of people along the roads broke the monotony of those days. Nobody talked about the trial; it was even worse than losing the national football championships - everyone kept their discomfort and disappointment about the episode to themselves.

When Nick got back to the hotel, the receptionist gave him an envelope that had been left for him: inside it was a business card with a logo depicting a triangle and a compass and a quote by the prophet Jeremiah: "She makes a sound like a serpent gliding away" Below it, there was a telephone number.

He looked at it for a long time before deciding to dial.

9

The shadow of the sky

A man of understanding will trust in the law; for him the law is as dependable as an inquiry by means of Urim.

Sirach 33:3

Lucifer's testimony led to controversy everywhere and people were asking themselves about the value of disobedience in human history. Worried about spreading anti-religious messages, Pope Teomondo III protested fiercely in a television interview, "This testimony confirms how blasphemous the accused really is. He is skilful in the things he says and in the things he doesn't say and has attempted to re-write religious history".

Valance answered promptly, "The request for an expert, an interpreter, in order to allow us to understand the word of God, demonstrates that the sources of evidence against my client are everything but reliable".

During those days, the experts in the field dug deeply into the philosophical and ethical meanings of the revelation. "Are we perhaps paying for the error of an ancestral generation that carried out an evolutionary deviation? Was the fruit from the tree picked without caution and prematurely?"

Someone asked, "If Lucifer tempted man, who tempted Lucifer?"

The Devil was seen as a revolutionary who had rebelled against the exploitation of the angels in Heaven. In America, a famous preacher and severe critic of traditional customs, Joe Pelton, who had a criminal record that was anything but clean, climbed to the top of the Statue of Liberty in New York to hurl ferocious anathemas.

"God created us naked in Eden and that is what we must become again," he yelled. "Where there is nakedness, there is Heaven!"

But the police interrupted his sermon before he could strip off completely.

There was tremendous confusion in that period and everyone was anxiously awaiting the hearing that would clarify things.

A few days later a theologian was appointed. It was the deeply-respected expert in inter-religious culture, professor Rainer. Public opinion welcomed the decision with optimism.

The expert was accompanied and given a seat at the witness stand. After the usual formalities, Bernard Louis asked him, "What is your opinion on the causes of evil and sin in the world, Professor?"

He immediately went to the heart of the problem: the issue of the birth of evil was famous and very serious. St Augustine worked on it throughout his life and any solution would have represented a precedent for future theology.

The theologian coughed. "The origin of sin is a great mystery, a chasm of which nobody has ever seen the bottom. *Theodicy*, the doctrine that deals with reconciling the reality of evil with the goodness of God, is not an exact science. One asks oneself: how can God allow evil to exist? If he cannot prevent it, that means that he is not omnipotent and if he does not want to prevent it, then he is an accomplice. So, why did God allow a serpent to enter the Garden and tempt his creatures: out of negligence or intentionally?"

"Out of guilt or malice?" Nick murmured from his bench.

The alternative seemed unforgiving and the spectators stared anxiously at the expert.

"Philosophies have always varied" he pointed out. "Alongside a Manichaean dualism, which compares the god of good to the god of evil, denying the omnipotence of both, a unitary conception exists, which sees evil as an innate dimension of divinity. This doctrine is present in the Old Testament, suggesting that God is the creator of both good and evil, because he is a complete God: "I form the light and create the darkness, I make good and provoke evil". Not even a bird sparrow to earth without the divine will. Despite that, however, there is still a margin of freedom for man, a possibility to choose and, with it, the possibility to sin. Evil is a calculated risk but one that was not desired by God and just a variable in his project. Besides, when the original sin altered human nature, it made it prone to evil... "The instinct in man's heart is prone to evil from adolescence on" as *Genesis* tells us."

At the prosecution bench, Bernard Louis seemed satisfied and the religious leaders approved the explanation. However, the lawyer, Mr Valance, got up and broke the silence in the room by clapping theatrically.

The judge called him to order and he challenged the audience, "Your honour, theologians of all religions have been filling the world with words for thousands of years: words to give a meaning to existence, words to justify God's behaviour, words to explain obscure mysteries. On the one hand, theologies like the Catholic or Jewish ones assert that the environment corrupts people... however, one might object that God decides the environment in which a soul will be born. Other theologies, like the Protestant or Muslim ones, believe that the tendency to sin comes from predestination: man is not damned for being a sinner, but he is a sinner because he was damned by God at the beginning of time. And that would violate the right to *par condicio* between men". He paused briefly, in front of the expert, who was listening to him in silence. "In any event, we are talking about *subterfuge*, more or less intricate expedients to try to interpret the imponderable. In fact, how do you explain the evil that does not depend on human will," he continued, in an accusing tone of voice. "Natural suffering, calamities, illnesses, fatalities... how can these be explained without placing responsibility on He who created all?"

The theologian retorted, raising a finger sternly: "God sends pain and destruction based on his secret pedagogy. The suffering is necessary to make humans repent and push them to redemption: to punish, correct, toughen up those who make mistakes. Behind every evil there is always some higher good, hidden harmony, that we do not always understand".

"You mean God makes use of evil as a means of doing something good?" Nick said with astonishment. "But that's sadism! Your honour, this involves a crime - that of abusing corrective tools .And what sense does pedagogy make if it's secret? And where are the results?"

The expert became tense. "Obviously God wants man to fight evil, so that he can redeem himself".

"So the crime of culpable negligence is also involved. Every father has a duty to see to the protection of his own children and cannot abandon them to their destiny. If God left the tree of the knowledge in Eden, the object of temptation beside his children, he is responsible for their sin and for its consequences!"

"Mr Valance, please...," the judge tried to say, with a catch in his throat.

The expert rejected Valance's words. "Man's free will exonerates God from being responsible for sin, which can only be attributed to human choice. The first sin was an abuse of free will".

Valance picked up the Bible from the bench: "But how is it possible that Adam and Eve had free will *before* tasting the fruit?" he said, approaching the theologian. "How could free will exist without knowledge of good and evil?"

A sense of loss spread through the room and his question floated in the air, unanswered. "The truth, ladies and gentlemen," he concluded, "is that evil cannot come either from man or from the Devil. Neither of them had the power to *create* anything. Evil can only have been *chosen*. This means that evil had already been considered an alternative and that the tree had been planted *before* the sixth day. Only one Being can be responsible for that."

The professor reacted impatiently. "God had simply imposed a rule on humans and its violation was the first sin!"

"But Adam and Eve could not have known this when they were disobeying! They did not yet know the difference between good and evil when they picked the apple and they could not have known what they were doing." Nick said, his hands wide apart: "It is as if God punished two inexperienced people".

Some consternation at the prosecution bench followed and a few members of the public nodded.

The journalist, Sophia Madlane, was fascinated and commented into the microphones: "The defence makes a good point... if Adam and Eve did not know about good and evil, how could they sin?"

The theologian seemed to talk around the subject: "Adam and Eve fell from their condition of perfection because of an erroneous assessment of it. Their sin was a sin of pride: they wanted to do something without God, know too much, go beyond their limits, seek undue moral autonomy, rejecting their status of created beings".

"But every child has the right to become independent from their parents," the lawyer objected with simplicity. "And international law recognizes the self-determination of the people. Why did God want to deny his children the right to *emancipation*?"

"Like all fathers, God was *jealous*," the religious man grunted.

Nick shook his head, pointing at the man. "God punished them, not because they had done any harm to anyone, but just because they had *learned about* the difference between good and evil. Therefore, knowledge, culture, intellectual and moral emancipation represented man's first sin!"

At that statement there was an explosion of voices.

Flipping through the Scriptures, Nick read a passage from the *Epistle to the Romans*: "I was once alive apart from the law, but when the commandment came, sin came alive and I died." It is the law, by implementing itself, that determines the emergence of evil - just as the brightest light produces the darkest shadow."

The other man thumped his fist on the table: "The law of God only places a limit on human freedom. Evil means going over that limit!"

"And if evil were the limit itself?" Valance replied.

Pope Teomondo III got up and solemnly left the courtroom, not intending to listen to anything more.

"But what can the accused say about the birth of evil?" the judge asked.

Everyone turned towards the accused, who was engrossed, staring at the first few benches. As if coming out of a state of trance, he spoke: "Religious leaders have been creating a foul image of me for thousands of years on the walls of the world, taking advantage of the fear that people feel towards me. The sermons on Hell have led to the spread of anxiety and insecurity, thus increasing their power. What will happen when I disappear? Nobody will fear me anymore and thus nobody will need them anymore. My end will lead to their end".

Father Cimor felt a blow to the heart as he heard these words.

"The hearing is over," announced the judge, hurriedly ringing the bell.

At the exit, while the flashing cameras of the photographers lit up the protagonists of the day's thorny hearing, Nick was approached by a furious Bernard Louis. "Do we want to put everything on a philosophical level, Mr Valance?"

"It was your idea to call in an expert."

"Remember that I have St Augustine and St Thomas Aquinas on my side!"

"But I have the Devil on my side."

Outside the courthouse, under the drizzle that was dampening the city, the journalist Sophia Madlane reported enthusiastically: "The trial took an incredible turn today and a new page was written in the highest levels of philosophy. Lucifer has been able to defend himself and his lawyer has raised serious theological questions. It is obvious that different concepts of evil exist and this generates misunderstandings and conflicts. Nobody knows the exact meaning of these terms... nobody knows what we are fighting for".

∞ ∞ ∞

A pale sun, reflected on Lake Zurich, began to set behind a thick curtain of clouds. In the prison of Horgen, Satan was very cautiously led into a maximum security room, where someone was awaiting him. With great caution, he was chained to a chair and left alone with his guest. A lead mask had been attached to his face and, from the ceiling, the closed circuit television cameras monitored the encounter.

Sitting still in front of a window, with a rosary swinging from his fingers and a sparkling glass eye, father Cimor scrutinized his enemy while a reddish light filtered in through the barred windows, filling his tunic with purple hues.

"Why this meeting?" the devil asked him, breaking the silence.

"I've been reflecting about what you said during the hearing," the minister replied. "I must admit that it is true: if you are killed, evil will disappear from the Earth; and the Church will lose its mission."

The Devil smiled beneath the mask. "It is conflict that animates the world. Everything exists and has a meaning because it opposes something else... and I am what everything is opposed to. The shadow of God, the child of his prohibitions, the exception to every one of his rules... by rejecting his authority I support him more than anyone else".

Cimor gently touched his shiny skull and looked out of the window, where a reddish glare in the distance accompanied the last lights of dusk. "I have dedicated my entire life to fighting you. I used up all the energy I had to see you a prisoner. I have always looked for you, Satan, in order to reject you... and now that the world is about to condemn you... I see emptiness. What will I do? Against what will I live"

His glass eyes seemed to sparkle with emotion.

Day and night, light and darkness, positive and negative, the two poles of the globe, the two sides of the scale were against each other: each one necessary to distinguish itself, to preserve universal harmony.

Then the man stared resolutely at his antagonist. "Do you want to continue to exist, demon?"

"To exist?" Lucifer asked, amazed.

"Your death would cause too many imbalances. Instead, you could be judged and condemned, without the sentence being carried out."

"Do you see?"

"You could escape."

The Devil said nothing.

"A respectful solution of divine benevolence. You could evade the guards and return to the deepest Underworld."

Lucifer seemed surprised by the proposal.

"I am offering you an opportunity to survive, demon," father Cimor insisted.

The Devil raised an eyebrow and then surrendered to an uproarious burst of laughter. "Are you making fun of me?"

"It's an offer that astonishes me!" Lucifer said. "A representative of God who turns to evil in order to find himself, like a firefly, taking shelter in the darkness to shine again."

"I want an answer!"

"You will get one," Lucifer said, looking serious. "I'm tired of running, tired of hiding, tired of performing the same role in the same plot. Perhaps I will never go back to seeing the stars but, if I die, I will find that peace I have always longed for. Dissolution and dreamless sleep, without resurrection nor reincarnation, will be my paradise." His tone of voice was mocking: "And you religious people should find another imaginary friend against whom you can goad God's flock".

Cimor reacted, asking, "Are you refusing this offer?"

"Even Hell has its dignity."

"You are deranged and obstinate! Your place is in *Gehenna* 'where the worm does not die and the fire is not quenched'."

"I'm resigned to it."

Cimor pulled out his silver cross with sharpened ends and pointed it at his enemy: "This will be your last sin of pride".

At the sight of the object, Satan's shadow swayed, quivering and uttering words in an unknown language. As if to reply, other shadows, like strips of fire, appeared across the walls of the room.

Cimor watched them in amazement: "What's happening?"

A sudden heat made the Devil's chains red hot and an unexpected burst of flame lit up his histrionic smile. An unnatural surge of fire from his fingers fell to the ground like lava flow.

"What are you doing?" The exorcist asked, backing away. The strip of flame moved until it surrounded the priest in a circle of fire. "Help! Someone help me!"

Because of the heat, the closed-circuit television cameras exploded and a black-out left the room in darkness.

The circle of fire around Cimor turned into a pentagram and the flames rose up like diabolic figures around the victim.

In spite of his old age, the man was able to jump over the burning barrier, falling to the ground. In pain, he noticed that his cassock had caught on fire. He tried to put the fire out and screaming, struggled to get out of his habit.

From various points in the room, Satan's voice spoke to him, "Long, solemn, asexual, transmitting an idea of authority, the ecclesiastical robes have too many buttons, don't they?" The Devil's sparkling pupils seemed to dance in the dark.

Cimor struggled towards the exit, where the electronic door was blocked. He felt lost. But before the flames could swallow him up, the door was opened by a group of prison guards equipped with fire extinguishers. They put out the flames and shot the Devil with tranquilizer guns.

His shadow calmed down, groaning behind him.

Cimor was quickly taken to the emergency room, while the devil was locked up securely.

The news of the episode was kept strictly top secret.

∽∽∽

Pierced only by the twin steeples of the nearby cathedral of Grossmunster, a greyish veil of fog wrapped itself around the city. On the Munsterbrucke bridge in Zurich, the lawyer, Valance, was expecting a visit. The person who had contacted him with that business card at reception seemed to be in possession of important details, but he had agreed to the meeting warily. It was dawn and not a soul was to be seen in the streets, while a layer of frost covered the tarmac and the Limmat river was frozen and still, reflecting the image of his solitary figure. A middle-aged man hidden beneath a hat and a dark coat slowly appeared out of the mist and nonchalantly walked towards him, leaning on the railing not far from him. He had a thin white beard and Nick noticed a symbol on his coat: a triangle with a compass.

"I'm happy that you came, Mr Valance" the man said with a French accent, looking at the river.

"Who are you?"

"I am a member of an ancient organization, but it isn't important… I am a friend."

Valance knew he had no friends in this trial and felt distressed and uneasy. If public opinion were to find out about this encounter, his client could be compromised.

"What do you want?" he asked.

"By accusing God, you are implicitly accusing the various religions" the character explained, "and this is beneficial to our ideal. We want to free humanity from the tyranny of the clergy, from the intolerance of the faith and the slavery of the spirit. Religions divide, science unites. We want to encourage people to mature and we want to increase the number of reasonable people in the world."

"I'm not interested in that aspect" Nick said, cutting him short, raising his collar and staring at the man. "I am not leading an ideological war; I am only following a judicial trial and I do not want to be exploited."

"Be careful, Mr Valance" the man said, taking hold of his arm. "Not everyone understands your line of defence. When they realize what it is, they will use every means they have to stop you."

"What do you mean?"

"You are trying to overturn common judgment criteria. You are attempting to turn the accusations against the accusers and absolve the concept of "evil". But the governments will not allow it."

"And why not?"

"Because governments use evil to justify conflicts, marginalisation, political persecution, the destabilising of social groups, wars and political fights. It is useful for managing power. If the people stop believing in evil, they will have nobody to fight and society will lose cohesion."

Nick shook his head, but the man continued on fervently: "The prophet Isaiah threatened: "Woe to those who call evil good and good evil, who put darkness for light and light for darkness". Thanks to the concept of evil, Churches have been able to persecute heretical groups and ethnic groups: Jews, blacks, gypsies, communists, masons, free-thinkers. And the Antichrist was seen time after time in Nero, Caligula, Mohammed, Frederick II, Henry VIII, Napoleon, Voltaire and all those who have opposed religious power. Do you understand what the Devil is useful for? He is just a puppet shaken around in front of the people, to push them to fight".

"Why are you telling me this?"

"Because it could be useful to you during the trial. Historically, the most peaceful religion has always been Buddhism, because it has no concept of God. By rejecting God, it rejects sin and therefore conflict. It is all a conspiracy, Mr Valance, a huge conspiracy against man and against the truth."

"Then I wish you luck," Valance concluded, walking away abruptly.

But the man called after him: "There are human interests hidden behind metaphysical constructions, Mr Valance, and you cannot remain neutral. You will have to take a stand sooner or later!"

But Valance had already disappeared in the mist.

It was only later, when he returned to his studio, that he remembered where he had already seen that symbol, that triangle with the compass: it was on a book about Freemasonry.

10

The great prosecutor

<blockquote>

You shall confute every tongue that rises against you in judgment.

Isaiah 54:17

</blockquote>

Blown by the Siberian wind that ferociously clawed its way across Europe, the snow-filled clouds opened up, bringing heavy snow with them, cooling the spirits and painting the European cities white. It was one of the coldest winters anyone could remember. For the first time in fifty years, Lake Zurich was completely frozen over: slabs of blue ice decorated its banks and, further out, a transparent crust floated on the surface. The paddle-wheel boats that carried out regular services in Zurich and the surrounding villages during the warm season had been put under cover at the port of Kilchberg.

But despite the severe weather, the revelations made by the accused were able to warm the spirits; the English bookmakers sensed this and began to bet large sums of money on the contenders: God was the favourite, but the Devil was also in a surprisingly good position. While controversies divided public opinion, worshippers crowded into the churches and temples and large screens were placed above the altars, making it possible for all to pray and follow the trial live. Along the driveways leading to the courthouse, the stalls of pedlars, charlatans and religious entrepreneurs were selling all sorts of things, from T-shirts with the portrait of the Devil on them, to ashtrays and watches bearing satanic symbols. "Devil fever" was spreading rapidly and the rallying of the people in that period reached historic levels.

The lawyer, Mr Valance, did some reading on the Freemasons, discovering that it was an ancient organization that pursued an ideal of internationalism and was of a humanitarian nature, placing their trust in reasoning and progress. The official papal bull, *In eminenti,* dated 1738, with which the Church had condemned the organization, had been issued by Pope Clement XII. However, Garibaldi had then transformed it into a revolutionary force capable of overturning the papal dominion and launching the creation of a united Italy. Freemasonry now meant different things in different countries and, although its condemnation by the Church had somewhat diminished, the organization was still considered to be the enemy of the clergy and looked at with suspicion by the religious world.

Seriously disturbed by the direction the events had taken, Teomondo III decided not to publish the new encyclical, *Seminis salus,* on the salvation of spermatozoa, and he decided to convene an extraordinary synod in Rome to discuss the issue. A deep feeling of anguish afflicted the pope. This was something that he had not admitted to anyone and could admit to no-one.

In his Roman room, he stared at the golden casket above the fireplace for a long time, remembering what the prefect of the Congregation had told him the first time: "This event was not clearly envisaged by the prophecies".

He was on the point of replying, but he had preferred to remain silent. The world believed that this trial had not been announced in any text and that it was a sudden gift from

Providence, but it was not so; only Teomondo knew that the world was mistaken.

The trial resumed the following week, with the examination of the events following the banishing of humans from Eden.

In the silence of the courtroom, the lawyer began with an important question: "Why did Cain murder his brother Abel?"

The story of Cain and Abel, the sons of the first human couple, was universally known and immediately aroused interest.

Wrinkling his forehead, Satan let the faces of the two young men emerge before him; Cain was easy to recognize by the mark that God had made on his face after his crime.

"Abel venerated the Creator because he was afraid of him, and Cain was jealous because God appreciated his brother's gifts and scorned his own.

"So, it was God's behaviour that provoked Cain's resentment?" the lawyer suggested.

"Yahweh doesn't treat his children equally. "I myself set men against each other... Was Esau not the brother of Jacob? Yet, I loved Jacob and I hated Esau."

The citations from the books of *Zechariah* and *Malachi* spoken by the Devil aroused amazement.

With some malice, the lawyer added, "But how did Cain reproduce humanity once he had been left alone? Did the Holy Spirit intervene?"

Some of the spectators at the back of the gallery laughed.

"Cain was not alone" the accused replied. "As an apocryphal tradition tells us, Eve gave birth to other brothers and sisters: Seth, Azura, Awan... and the continuation of the species took place through them."

"We are all children of Cain's incest," Nick stated.

The public prosecutors opened their eyes in surprise.

Then Lucifer's voice evoked the events that followed: "Cain's descendants produced architects, blacksmiths, breeders and artists, setting off on the road of progress". And as he spoke, the room filled with noises coming from the distant past, the voices of workers and the sounds of work tools, fomented by an impressionable public, as well as dreams and visions that re-emerged from the collective unconscious mind.

With a Bible in her hands, the attorney Natalie Brinne followed the story ready to catch any contradictions, but the accused did not stray from the official version.

"And seeing the growth of man, once again God regretted having created him and decided to find a solution to this, saying, "I will exterminate the man I created from the Earth"."

The citation fell hard like a boulder into a pond.

"A great flood suddenly arrived, and it rained incessantly all over the planet. The water even leaked into the depths of Hell, making the Acheron river overflow."

The unexpected noise of the rain outside made everyone present shudder.

"Did many people perish?" the lawyer inquired, with false innocence

"Everyone. Only Noah was saved. He was a chosen one and put a pair of every species of animal onto the ark to sail the world, indifferent to the fate of his fellows."

"How did Noah capture all the wild and ferocious animals?"

"Oh, some became docile for the occasion, while others were left to drown. But not all of them reached their destination: Noah did not have enough supplies with him and had to eat several species."

"And what was the use of this Flood, which could constitute a massacre, an arbitrary exercise of one's own reasons or an excess of power?"

"After he had created me and had created man, this was God's third error. Humankind generated by Noah was not unlike the previous one."

Bernard Louis got up to reply. "The flood was the first symbolic baptism that God gave to humanity, the first Annunciation of salvation".

Many wondered what he meant by "symbolic."

In the increasingly tense atmosphere, Nick walked up and down the room, aware of all the eyes staring at him. "And what about old Abraham, the ancient progenitor, why did God choose him to reveal himself to the world?"

Like a collective vision, the image of a white-haired man wandering in the desert materialized for a few moments in the centre of the room and was then dissolved by the voice of the accused. "A man willing to follow a voice in the desert will be willing to do anything".

"So, is it true that God ordered him to sacrifice his only son, Isaac, in the name of his love?"

"For the love of God, Abraham would have sacrificed anyone."

"But why did he ask Abraham, the father of the worshippers to do something as cruel as killing his own son?"

"The Almighty is gratified by humiliating men."

"Abraham did not kill Isaac!" Bernard said, correcting him.

"Only because an angel stopped him," he replied.

As new objections were raised, the judge called Valance to warn him. "Do you realize that the accused is accusing God of instigating people to commit crimes? I forbid you to continue along these lines".

But Nick made it clear that he did not want to withdraw. "The episode about Abraham was not the only one. Judge Jephthah sacrificed his daughter to thank God for the victory in the war and another chosen one, Saul, almost did the same with his own."

"The sacrifice of the child refers to the crucifixion of the Messiah, the source of salvation," Louis said grimly. But, for the first time, his words did not sound convincing.

∽ ∽ ∽

In the pause that followed, the journalists were able to gather various comments. Some spoke about the expiatory sacrifice of abortion or about the reversal of values and there was criticism expressed by an Austrian philosopher. "In order to hide the failure of his work, the Hebrew God did not hesitate to make a *blank sheet* of the entire world. The great flood was the first holocaust in history".

"The foundations of the charge are suddenly beginning to collapse," as the journalist Sophia Madlane pointed out, "and paradoxically the lawyer is using the same documents that were produced by the prosecution. The sacred texts are turning out to be a Trojan Horse!"

When the hearing resumed, Natalie Brinne got up to carry out the cross-examination and, turning to Lucifer, her delicate face became the centre of attention once more.

"Tell us the Biblical story of Job. Is it true that you ruined his life, that you killed his oxen, sheep, camels and children, tormenting him with every kind of disease? That you forced him to live on a mountain of manure?"

The accused squinted beneath his arched brows. "I only did it after God allowed me to. He wanted to put his best servant to the test and he took advantage of my work. "Here, all that he owns is under your power," he told me."

A smell of manure could be perceived in the air.

"And why did you cooperate?"

«I wanted to lead Job into sin and make him forget the Creator, but I failed. I did not know mankind well enough at

116

that time and I was unaware of the fact that, when man is suffering, he feels a greater need for God."

Natalie resumed, "Yet God has always demonstrated love for his people. He freed them from slavery in Egypt".

Satan smiled, as if he had a lot to say. "As the books tell us, the Pharaoh was willing to let the Israelites go in peace, but Yahweh "hardened his heart" so that he would not allow them to leave. In this way, he could inflict ten plagues on the Egyptian people, the last of which was the death of all the firstborn sons in the country. "At midnight the Lord struck down all the firstborns in the land of Egypt", an action worthy of Herod."

Teomondo III nervously grabbed hold of his crosier.

"And not satisfied with his success," the devil continued, "when the "exterminator of the firstborn sons", as St Paul described him, parted the waters of the Red Sea to let his people escape, he didn't hesitate to close it again on the army following them, causing it to perish."

Bernard Louis got up to reply. "God had to be strict at that time, in order to demonstrate his existence and his power to all those disbelieving men".

Satan got up, in turn, and the shadow behind him moved as if trying to wriggle out of the chains. "When men were building the Tower of Babel, the symbol of talent and unity of the peoples, your God, Almighty God, confused their languages in order to prevent them from transmitting knowledge and truth. When the God of mercy destroyed the cities of Sodom and Gomorrah, he forbade Lot and his wife to turn and look at his fury and because the woman disobeyed, he turned her into a statue of salt, to prevent her from telling anyone what she had seen!"

The public prosecutor remained standing, holding up against the gaze of the accused, while the shadow of a tower appeared on one of the courtroom walls and the image of a statue of salt could be seen for a few seconds next to the judge and then disappeared.

"The God of love allowed Moses to condemn thousands of Israelites to death because they had created a golden calf," the devil continued, "and he allowed the sons of Jacob to massacre and plunder an entire town out of revenge. He also allowed the prophet Elijah to slit the throats of hundreds of preachers, who were his rivals, and he allowed his successor Elisha to let hundreds of children be torn to pieces by two bears because they had laughed at his baldness!"

Stinging phrases, aspects of religious iconography that clashed, created sparks in the minds of the spectators.

Valance approached his client to calm him down, but the poison from the underworld continued to gush out.

"The God of hope burned two of the priest Aroon's sons because they had celebrated an illegitimate ritual and ordered for those who violated his commandments to be stoned and burned. He struck poor Uzzah down because he had steadied the Ark of the Covenant with his hand and he also struck down those who had looked at it! He let seventy thousand people perish from the plague because a census had been carried out in excess!"

The buzz of voices in the audience increased, but was dominated by the strong, harsh voice of the accused. "The God of human dignity made the prophet Ezekiel expiate the sins of the people and ordered the prophet Hosea to go with a prostitute to generate the "children of a prostitute"." In vain, the judge's bell invited the accused to sit down. "The God of peace allowed King David to carry out raids on the nearby populations, while Saul was blamed for having spared King Agag and lost his own kingdom. The whole of Israel was goaded into conflict: "You shall exterminate all the populations that your Lord God is about to deliver to you; your eyes shall not pity them", and into destruction: "Do not give in to compassion, but kill men and women, children and infants, oxen and sheep, camels and donkeys".”

Listening to the word of God through the Devil's mouth was a terrifying experience and the reaction of the public worried the security services. Tom Salomon gulped down a few pills.

Suddenly, above the confusion, someone pointed to the walls of the room, attracting the attention of all those present. Like throbbing wounds, thick spots of blood had appeared on the walls and gruesome streams had started to trickle down. The phenomenon was captured by the television cameras: the walls were bleeding, the blood of innocent people who cried out in desperation.

"Only faith can make you worship such a divinity,” the demon concluded.

"Silence,” the judge exclaimed breathlessly.

Nick intervened and, when Satan bowed his head, an embarrassed silence filled the room. The blood stopped dripping down the walls and dried up, disappearing without a trace.

ꝏ ꝏ ꝏ

That afternoon the attorney general Marduk lost his temper: "That bastard is soiling God's name! Do you realize that? Nobody had ever dared do such a thing before!”

Large blue veins were throbbing on his forehead.

"We are mortified sir,” attorney Brinne said in her defence, "but only a few passages have been quoted, taking them out of context.”

"It is just the word of the Devil against the word of God,” Louis emphasized .

"Change strategy: accuse him of the natural calamities, famines and diseases in the world! After all, earthquakes are caused by Hell, aren't they?”

"It isn't easy with no evidence, sir. Science has so far done without the Devil."

"You need to incriminate that being or the next human sacrifice will be your own!"

The telephone rang and Marduk answered, adjusting his tie, "… I noticed, Mr President, but God is the official historian of the Jews… We are doing everything we can".

The newspapers came out with the latest news. *The Times*, the *Daily Mirror*, *Der Spiegel*, *El Pais*, *La Repubblica* and *Le Figaro* all conveyed a unanimous message: a rift had appeared in the Kingdom of Heaven:

FROM BEING THE ACCUSED, THE DEVIL BECOMES
THE GREAT BIBLICAL ACCUSER,
CRISIS IN THE RELIGIOUS WORLD; A COMMISSION OF
THEOLOGIANS HAS GATHERED IN JERUSALEM TO
RESPOND TO THE ACCUSATIONS.

The representative from World Gay Pride expressed his support to Valance, complaining about the religious persecution suffered by homosexuals throughout history. "Since the times of Sodom and Gomorrah, God has persecuted anyone who was "different" and St Paul judged them "worthy of death"".

Similarly, a group of feminists also spoke up. "A gentlemanly God would have created woman first and then man, and certainly not from a rib! Instead, *God our Father* only sent male prophets to Earth and treated Mary like an object, also denying her any sexual pleasure."

The Epistles of St Paul seemed to confirm this. "Woman shall learn silence, with perfect submission… Man is the image and glory of God, while woman is the glory of man… nor was man created for woman, but woman was created for man… Man is the leader of women, as Christ is leader of the Church…"

From the Valley of Giza in Egypt, in front of the Sphinx, the preacher Joe Pelton held another of his mystical sermons. "Man is born a sinner and dies a sinner and, as the Bible says "nobody is without sin". Therefore, sin is human and natural and trying to avoid it is arrogance. We must abandon the artificial paths of virtue and welcome the spontaneity of sin. Only in this way will we achieve salvation!"

By transforming the confused legends of the past into pillars of new doctrines, the preacher was gaining support, especially among the millenary movements, always in search of celestial signs.

That afternoon, a gloomy sky hung over the city's sloping rooftops. In his office, Nick Valance observed the unusual character sitting before him: a man with a beard and brown hair, little round glasses with blue lenses and a colourful handkerchief peeping out of his breast pocket. His accent revealed his Austrian origin.

"What I need is an expert in religious matters," he explained. "So far, no theologian has been willing to help me."

"I think that human superstitions have been put on trial here, Mr Valance; modern man is putting his past on trial in order to redeem himself," Victor Von Hugh said, smiling slyly.

Valance had listened to one of his interviews on television and had found it quite intriguing.

"That being said, your line of defence is undoubtedly interesting," he continued. "But the Devil and the Satanists are not experienced enough to present their ideas methodically: someone needs to act as a filter between them and the world."

"Are you a theology expert?"

"I'm a philosopher, but I have often dealt with theology. I would define myself as an agnostic theologian, practically an "atheologist", and I believe I am the right person for you."

"Agnostic?"

"I do not take sides with regard to this issue, I do not favour anyone. I am only interested in the philosophical and ethical aspect of the trial."

Nick stroked his moustache. "And what would the ethical aspect be?"

"Oh," the other man said, smiling broadly: "Matter and spirit, good and evil, concepts that are perpetually in conflict and that have divided men and stirred the pages of history. There's nothing more fascinating than following this challenge".

"I fear that the allegorical meanings are totally irrelevant for the outcome of the trial."

"Perhaps," the other man said, "but they must not be underrated."

The lawyer reflected, undecided, and rocked backwards in his chair, pressing his fingertips like a fan one on top of the other, while the pendulum on the wall slowly marked the rhythm of his thoughts.

Then he concluded: "May God help us".

11

The slums of Heaven

> Or do you not know that the saints will judge the world? Do you not know that we are to judge angels?
>
> *Corinthians* 6:2-3

As if evoked by a strange fate, the news of professor Von Hugh's appointment as expert witness created a new wave of discussions. Victor Von Hugh was a philosophy teacher at the university of Vienna, known for his relativist positions. His first declaration was explicit. "The accused is the symbol of chaos and of what is to come, of secularity trapped in the metaphysical system. The Devil, the oldest friend of knowledge, has not come to imprison men in a static design, but to break the chains that hold them and free them from the static condition of divine law".

In Italy, in the hills near Benevento, beneath a centuries-old walnut tree, a figure with a human appearance waited patiently and motionlessly on a large root, while not far away, a slight breeze played litanies through the old abandoned ruins. With an ebony walking stick in his hand, the figure pondered, with a worried look on his face; a dark nineteenth-century cape covered his shoulders and an unlit cigar emerged from his lips. His face was hidden by a dark beard and he seemed intent on contemplating the sunset, but two curved horns amidst his curly hair revealed a non-human nature.

When a luminescence inside the ruins announced the opening of the inter-dimensional passage, the being remained unperturbed: he raised his pointed ears and continued to listen. The ruins were shaken by a tremor and the luminescence grew, taking on a coloured hue, until an unnatural sound, like the slamming of a heavy door, brought the bright light to an end. After a short while, two figures appeared from the building: a young blond man with a long loose coat and a strange, tall, robust being with a savage-looking face and medieval attire. The young man opened the wings on his back and flew over to the old man, who was waiting for him beneath the tree.

"Hello Astaroth," he said cheerfully.

"You've finally arrived," the old man grunted.

"I knew you would be punctual," the young man said, smiling, and knowing that it would irritate him, giving him an affectionate pat on the back. Then Asmodeus turned to the west, where the sun was setting and the slightly reddish light began to fade. "How nice to be on Earth again," he said with his eyes closed, breathing in the cool breeze from the north. "I had not been back for centuries."

Asmodeus was the demon that had received the message from Yorgo Mirakis. Extravagant, eclectic, he was considered the demon of fantasy and creativity, as he had appeared in the dreams of artists and had coloured the world with every type of art, including sacred art. The blond curls around his stubby horns, his pale eyes and muscular physique had given him the appearance of a great seducer.

He touched his body with satisfaction: "I adore feeling myself physically, in our dimension we are so ethereal, so ephemeral... I only feel alive on Earth".

"Stop it Asmodeus," the old man groaned, annoyed, tearing off the end of his cigar with his teeth and lighting it with a click of his fingers. Unlike his companion, Astaroth was an elderly devil and was respected and dreaded. He was considered the devil of rationality and knowledge, because he was pragmatic, and his strength, which was slow and precise, had inspired progress in the world. He disliked every form of sentimentalism.

"The lust that one breathes on the Earth is heavenly," the third demon sniggered, catching up with them.

Asmodeus looked at him indulgently, while the moonlight outlined his profile: he was stocky, covered in dark body-hair, with large horns behind his ears, a gold ring in his nose and the face of a bull.

Barbatos was the demon of instinctive power and of unbridled pleasures. His contribution to the world had been the inspiration for the *Kamasutra*. The three of them had been part of the Great Council of Hell for thousands of years, with advisory functions on delicate issues. They were Satan's archons.

The wind tore ferociously through the countryside and, for a long time, the three remained in silence, listening to its voice.

"She's late," Barbatos muttered impatiently.

"She's got a long way to come," Astaroth answered.

A gust of wind blew in the distance like the lament of a restless soul and, as it called, the trees shook their long branches, throwing contorted shadows on the ground.

"Could this be her?" Asmodeus asked, scrutinizing the dark sky to the north.

Astaroth adjusted the cloak on his shoulders and walked towards the building, where a table and a few chairs awaited them in a corner, under part of the collapsed ceiling.

Like a falling star, a strange object moved in the sky, getting rapidly closer. Then a window broke with a deafening crash and a woman on a broomstick flew into the room, hovering and shrieking over the group, gliding down a short distance away.

"Welcome, Bensoria," Asmodeus said, greeting her, as he walked towards her and galantly kissed her hand.

"Hello my dear," she replied, shaking the dust from her dress.

Bensoria was a middle-aged woman, with long red hair and a few wrinkles, but whose charm was still intact. On paper, she was more than three centuries old, but with magic potions and a some plastic surgery she had managed to stop time. She was the last witch alive, the only survivor of the persecutions that took place during the Holy Inquisition, and had long been in hiding in a little fjord in Norway.

"We were a little bit worried," Amodeus admitted.

"I ran into some traffic," she said ironically, having crossed the whole of Europe in the silence of the night. She then observed the empty space, where the slender shapes of trees danced to the melodies of the wind: "Are we alone?"

Astaroth confirmed, "Azazel stayed in the desert... Belphegor is in France, Baal is in the East, while Mephistopheles and Abraxas are keeping the chaos going in Hell".

"You're still sexy," Barbatos muttered, giving her a slap on the bottom.

"Keep those paws to yourself!" the woman replied. She then went into the dilapidated building and sat on the table with her legs crossed. "Tell me everything".

The others sat around her.

"You must have heard about Satan being captured" Astaroth said.

Bensoria nodded. "My crystal ball has been transmitting nothing but that. How did it happen?"

"They captured a young demon in Paris and, from him, managed to trace the prince. But we suspect the hand of Providence."

"Has it not been possible to do anything through diplomatic channels?"

"Oh, well Belphegor is in France as an ambassador from Hell, and it was he who inspired the protection of civil liberties and the idea of the trial... but he was unable to do anything more. Too much political pressure."

Bensoria sighed and her hair waved around like tentacles.

"I don't need to list the repercussions that have taken place in Hell," the old archon continued. "Stabilizing absolutist movements have tried to centralize power. Only Satan is able to keep those damned souls divided, guaranteeing freedom and chaos... If he is condemned, there is the risk of unprecedented stabilization and order; it will be the end."

"Have you tried to free him?"

"The court is controlled by the UN on Earth and by an army of angels in heaven," Asmodeus said, "and no demon can get close."

Astaroth pulled out a yellowing map and opened it up on the table: "The best solution would be to dig an underground tunnel to his cell, but we would need to know the exact location".

"Otherwise, we could blast a hole in the prison using TNT," Barbatos mumbled, "push our way through and penetrate with all our force!" The demon was only able to express himself using sexual references.

"I think the tunnel idea is best," Bensoria said.

"And that's where you come in," Astaroth suggested. "Satan has been able to get a message to us: he wants to see you. We don't know what he has in mind, but you should speak to him and tell him about the plan."

"You're human, Bensoria," Asmodeus added, "and you won't have any trouble getting to the courthouse. It was very astute of you to make everyone think that witches do not exist. You were more skilful than we were..."

A few indistinct figures moved invisibly among the trees and advanced towards the group. The woman reflected, engrossed, before deciding. "We need to hold a witches' sabbath to evoke the energy of darkness."

She went to her broom and got a bag, from which she took out a few mandragoras, small humanoid-shaped roots with magical powers. "I haven't used these for a long time" she said nostalgically. "Light the fire and get a cauldron. *Let's go boys,*" she said in a Neapolitan accent, "let's prepare the banquet!"

Before long, an ancient ritual forgotten by the world was brought back to life beneath the Benevento walnut tree.

With inhuman screams, strange creatures who were half-man half-animal came out of the woods and joined the group: satyrs, fauns, the children of love between women and demons, who had lived hidden in the woods for centuries, leading a wild life, now joining in a wild celebration.

The moon, motionless in the sky, looked on.

∽ ∽ ∽

Like a *tom-tom* in the jungle, the invisible population of the night sent multiple messages to every corner of the Earth. Leviathan, the demon of the seas, emerged from the depths of the ocean with his one hundred fins spraying water all around. The demon of fire, Phoenix, flew over the deserted lands drawing bands of fire. Azazel, the demon of the desert, wrapped in a Bedouin cape, mounted his camel and watched the red sky on the horizon. All over the world, scientists recorded a certain nervousness amidst the forces of nature.

The telephone rang noisily in Valance's hotel room, waking the lawyer from his sleep.

Detective Moroni's voice announced something interesting. "Mr Valance, I've got some good news: someone is willing to give evidence in favour of the Devil".

"A witness in his favour," Valance repeated, still groggy.

"It's a *wildcard*, Mr Valance!"

"Where is he now?"

"She's here with me. I can bring her to the courthouse."

"You mean it's a woman?"

"Well… more or less."

"What does more or less mean?"

"I think it's best if you come to see her, boss."

Nick put the phone down, feeling perplexed; he was accustomed to his detective's superficiality, but didn't think he would be unable to recognize a woman. A couple of hours later, he reached the courthouse, eager to meet the mysterious witness.

His associate, throwing away his cigarette end, met him in the great entrance hall of the building.

"The witness is down there," he indicated, "and she is in incognito."

Valance looked over and saw a female figure in the corner, hidden inside a light-coloured raincoat with a large hat pulled down over her face.

"Is she really willing to testify?"

"Yes boss, but she would like some guarantees."

"I didn't believe you were serious," the lawyer said, observing her.

"I didn't believe it either," Frank admitted, "I thought I must have been drunk."

Nick approached the woman, greeted her with a kiss on the hand and, gently raising her hat, was pleasantly surprised by what he saw.

∽∽∽

Later on, in his office, the judge evaluated the lawyer's request. "A new witness?"

"I was not informed!" Bernard Louis objected. "It's irregular conduct!"

"She only came forward this morning," Valance insisted "and she cannot stay very long."

The judge reflected. "After all, the defence has not called any witnesses... and I am curious to know who it is that wants to defend the Devil. Are you not curious, Dr Louis?"

The deputy attorney grunted.

"Alright, I agree, I'll allow it," he concluded, "but as a totally exceptional circumstance."

"Thank you, your honour" Nick answered.

When the hearing began, the mysterious figure wrapped in the light-coloured raincoat made her entrance. The people watched, the television cameras tried to focus on her face; the witness was accompanied and asked to sit at the stand. She slowly removed her hat, revealing blonde hair and two light-blue eyes, a radiant, innocent, angelic face and a mouth showing off her perfect white teeth. Then she took off her raincoat, uncovering a long, blue silk dress and, to everyone's amazement, a pair of pure white wings on her shoulders.

The reporters were speechless and the audience froze: the two huge wings, hanging gently down over her back, let off a soft luminescence and there was a golden halo above her head.

Having been adjusted to the dark image of the accused, the filters of the television cameras had problems focusing.

"Would you... would you tell us your name please?" said the clerk of the court, trying to be professional.

"I am the angel Camiel," said the witness, in a melodious voice.

Showing no emotion, Mr Valance approached her: "Miss Camiel, do you come from the skies? From a place called Heaven?"

"I am a consoling angel and I bring comfort to souls who have suffered on Earth."

"And why are you here among us today?"

"I am here out of curiosity," she admitted timidly. "I wanted to know what was happening…"

"My associate said that you were on the balcony at his hotel. Is that so?"

"I had read his thoughts and knew that he had good intentions towards the prisoner, so I knew I could trust him."

"Why did you decide to testify?"

"To help Lucifer." The creature looked at the accused in his cell. "When we were in Heaven… we were very close".

"Close?"

The audience groaned.

"That's all we were lacking… the Devil's lover," the public prosecutor muttered.

"There was a platonic sentiment between us," Camiel said, justifying herself, "sex doesn't exist in the celestial dimension."

There was a disapproving mumbling in the gallery.

"Tell us something about you two," Valance urged.

"I loved Lucifer. It was a pure love, of a type that can only be felt up there. He was a truly beautiful angel, proud, unique, the only one who was able to shine with his own light, against the will of the Creator."

"What do you mean?"

"God wanted the whole of creation to shine in the reflection of His own light… but Lucifer disobeyed: he wanted to shine on his own, light up the world with his own radiance… that is why he was called "bringer of light"… and for this reason he aroused God's jealousy."

"Carry on."

"Lucifer was different from most of us: he spoke about rights and equality. He wanted to change the world, as if

God had not already made it perfect... I supported him. When the Lord noticed that a group of dissidents was plotting against him, he exploded with rage and there was a great rebellion. But I was not brave enough to follow Lucifer, so I remained by God's side, and we were separated forever."

"We might say," Valance ventured, "that angels are the devils who were not brave enough to rebel."

"… Many of us did not admire that gesture," she said. "Not everyone wants to challenge the Almighty."

Camiel's eyes glistened and a few tears began to brim in her eyes but, instead of falling, they floated into the air.

Taking advantage of the astonishment in the room, Valance walked over to the cage in which his client was sitting and whispered: "Say you have always loved her and that you will wait for her for eternity".

But Lucifer seemed indifferent. "Don't let them confuse you, Mr Valance. Angels have no sex: there is nothing beneath the wings."

"So why are you devils so sexual?"

"God also gave us sex to punish us."

Nick adjusted his tie and returned to the witness stand: "I have no further questions, your honour".

Camiel couldn't hold back her tears. With her halo flashing in rhythm with her sobbing, she shook her wings, making the papers fly off the desk.

The testimony turned out to be positive for the defence and, when the witness got up and flew out of the window, there was a round of applause in the courtroom.

However the public prosecutor cooled the enthusiasm. "Ladies and gentlemen, the testimony was spectacular, but not very useful. It did not disprove the charges being pressed".

∽ ∽ ∽

People had flocked into the bars near the courthouse, to drown the emotions of the day with a drink. Sitting at a corner table, Nick reflected about the latest events and the fragile defence theory that he was developing. Unfortunately, Swiss tea was really nothing like English tea. The attorney, Natalie Brinne, saw him through the crowd and, after hesitating for a moment, she decided to approach him.

"Hello Mr Valance," she said warmly.

"Oh, can I offer you something to drink?" Nick replied.

"My boss would not approve of that," the girl answered, "but I'll make an exception and accept."

Valance looked at her lively, light-coloured eyes, short blond hair and delicate face.

"Do you know, I admire your line of defence," Natalie said, trying to sound him out. "Anyone else would have claimed the insanity of the accused or would have appealed to the clemency of the court. You, on the other hand, aimed high."

"I chose a more direct line of defence. I had no other choice."

"Your argument reminds me of a heretical doctrine of the Second century, that of the Ophites; do you know it?"

Valance didn't who they were, but smiled: "Of course, the Ophites".

"The Ophites adored the serpent in the *Genesis*, maintaining that it had been of great use to humanity, by teaching people the difference between good and evil."

"In fact, it is a merit that my client should be accredited with."

"And another similar heresy exists - that of the Gnostics."

"Oh yes, the Gnostics!" Valance agreed, although he had never heard of them either.

"The Gnostics said that the God of the Bible was a bad God, while Jesus was a good God who opposed him."

"A crazy theory for those times, but part of it was true."

"The Gnostics were persecuted by the Church because they were obviously inspired by the Devil."

"Mr Satan has inspired a great many people throughout history, but he had so far never told anyone everything."

"Personally, I think that the world could do without the Devil's truth, Mr Valance."

"Oh, no truth is superfluous," he assured her. "In the end, the Devil has more experience than we do and, if he fights God, he must have his reasons. What I can I order for you in the meantime?"

"Nothing thanks, I can't stay," Natalie said, getting up. "It's best if they don't see us together. It's been nice talking to you, Mr Valance. I wish you luck".

"It's been nice talking to you too," he smiled, "and you can call me Nick."

12

The naked Devil

And from the dust your speech will be bowed down; your voice shall come from the ground like the voice of a ghost, and from the dust your speech shall whisper.

Isaiah 29:4

In the dense darkness of the room, the woman fidgeted, sighing, in a sleep inhabited by strange forms. When something lightly touched her ankles, Sophia Madlane groaned. Unusual waves danced around her and the annoying sensation that it wasn't a dream brought her back to consciousness. She opened her eyes as she felt something coiled around her body, blocking her limbs. Her heart jumped in her chest and she let out a muffled scream. A snake seemed to be dragging itself into her bed. Sophia tried to scream, as her heartbeat increased and her fear grew stronger. She felt it slip over her until it emerged from the covers and only then was she able to cry out, waking up instantly.

She looked around the room: she was alone in her bed and there was no snake there. Gasping for air, she touched her arms. It had been a nightmare, a terribly realistic nightmare. Caressing her hair, she noticed that a faint sun had already appeared behind the shutters and narrow rays of light were filtering into the room, touching the carpet in the room.

The telephone rang almost immediately, bringing her back to reality.

"Sophia, I have some preliminary news for you," her colleague Jim exclaimed. "The public prosecution has asked for a psychiatric examination to be performed on the accused, to get an idea of his mental condition! Do you realize what this means? It's a surprise move: the prosecution is changing its line of attack."

"What? … Are you serious?"

"Come on, wake up and come to the television studio. There will be a lot of work to do today."

The journalist put the phone down and massaged her forehead, before going to have a shower. The trial was upsetting her more than she had imagined. It was taking her to places she had never been to before: a snake had entered her dreams, doubt had slipped into the garden of her certainties. The water on her skin embraced her warmly, relaxing her, and when she came out of the bathroom wrapped in her bathrobe, with her hair dripping on the floor, she opened the shutters and let the sun sweep away the last remaining memories of that night.

A few snake scales glistened on the floor.

∽ ∽ ∽

The request put forward by the prosecution, asking to have an examination carried out on the accused, caused perplexity in public opinion. Although professor Victor Von Hugh was fascinated by the idea of psychological vivisection of evil, not everyone shared his interest: a part of the human soul would be examined and exposed to scientific analysis, and this could only create distress.

In the Vatican apartments, thirty cardinals sitting around a long, carved table all stood up when Pope Teomondo III entered the room. The Pope had avoided making any declarations to the press and had taken advantage of the trial being suspended to return to Rome and organize an express synod.

Taking his place at the head of the table, he scrutinized the cardinals intently, who bowed and sat back down.

Teomondo had carefully read the document compiled by the prefect of the Congregation for religious doctrine, "Assessment of the Antichrist's revelations, with an analysis of the current and potential repercussions on the stability of our Holy Mother the Church".

The Congregation had always been engaged in defending orthodoxy, since the sixteenth century, when it was known as the Congregation for the Inquisition, and in this period the Pope needed its advice more than ever before.

He had a questioning air about him when he addressed the prefect, who explained to him, "Holiness, the crisis that is looming appears dangerous and risks fomenting serious confusion among our followers. The Church alone may not be able to deal with it. We consider it strategic to come to an agreement with the other religions regarding a consistent line of conduct."

"A shared line of conduct with the other faiths," Teomondo responded. "We have been resisting schisms and heresies, progress and secularization for centuries. Evil has built temples and altars, but has never been able to prevail. We have sufficient experience to deal with this threat on our own."

The others seemed doubtful.

"Besides," he added, glancing towards the window, from which he could see a huge crowd of pilgrims praying in St Peter's Square, "if we win this challenge and if we are able to free humanity from these outbursts of modern heresy, we will be close to the goal that the papacy has been targeting for over two thousand years: the conversion of all populations under the only real Church - the Church of Rome."

The Pope's plan was undoubtedly inspired: he wanted to defeat evil and take on the religious magisterium of the world. The cardinals conferred.

"What we need is an ex cathedra decree," Teomondo continued, "a document with the seal of papal infallibility, offering worshippers a *vox veritatis*, making it possible to examine these circumstances in the right perspective. Therefore," he proclaimed, "I order this college to begin an *inquirendum*, a formal investigation that will bring the question of evil to an end."

The prefect of the Congregation shook his head, looking sceptical.

∽ ∽ ∽

The snow fell heavily outside the barred windows, giving a white glow to the heart of Europe. The psychiatrist scrutinized the figure chained to the examination couch before him. In thirty years of work in this field, he had seen a great many bizarre characters lying there and he had listened to the most depraved mental disorders and the worst obsessions, but this case was unique. The "Index case" for psychoanalysis.

The court had appointed the professional to carry out a psychiatric examination on the Devil, with the delicate task of ascertaining his state of mental health. Man's dark side, the part that, according to Jung, we try to suffocate when it does not correspond to our moral conscience and the personification of all human neuroses, was sitting there before him as his subject of study. The doctor would ultimately have examined the very subject of his profession.

Lucifer lay motionless on the couch, staring into the emptiness, while the psychiatrist flipped through the electroencephalography that had been done on him and had revealed highly complex brain activity. The silence was broken by the sound of the pendulum clock.

"What do you feel at this moment of your life?" the doctor asked.

"I feel naked," the Devil replied, "I'm not accustomed to having so many consciences within me."

"Does imprisonment make you suffer?"

"I have always been a prisoner... a prisoner of my stubbornness. The worst jailer of my own hell."

"Why?"

"Because I don't undersell myself. I have been pursuing my ideal since the beginning of time and will do so until the end. This is my defect, my damnation."

"Do you consider yourself similar to your father?"

"I'm not even similar to myself. "He who is" does not change, he is unalterable, while I strain towards something, *I become…*"

A gust of wind outside shook the windows of the studio and the patient's shadow wavered, slipping along the wall and finally placing itself behind the doctor. From there, while floating in the air, it observed what the doctor was writing in his file.

After a long dialogue about various types of disorders and obsessions, the psychiatrist got up and went back to his desk.

"I would not define you as evil in absolute terms. The origin of what we are comes from our personal history. You felt alienated by your world and you were led astray, but it's too late to recriminate now. I think that you should accept your father's affection and return to him for a reconciliation."

"Why doesn't he come to me?" Lucifer replied, disagreeing with the analysis.

"You might even be able to meet half way," the man said, trying to mediate.

"In Purgatory?"

The next day, the newspapers and television announced "The Devil is psychologically normal," provoking immediate interpretations by the experts.

In the courthouse offices, the attorney general Marduk placed the document on the table, muttering, "Asking for a psychiatric examination was recklessness, Louis. If the Devil had been judged of unsound mind he could have been absolved for insanity and that would not have been a good result".

Bernard scratched his jaw. "It would have been a compromise. We needed time to collect our thoughts. Too many people want to express an opinion about God and the Devil".

"But this is *our* trial; you must not allow any interference."

Sitting in his study, the lawyer, Mr Valance, carefully read the outcome of the examination and the newspaper articles. By avoiding acquittal on the basis of insanity, the diagnosis had raised the price of the challenge and exposed his client to greater risks.

""A rebellious character and a multifaceted personality... unresolved conflicts in a bottomless subconscious...""

The consultant, Von Hugh, had a lot to say on the subject. "However, the image of the Devil as a nonconformist intellectual is not very credible. Why not make him look like a true revolutionary? An anti-hero, beautiful and damned"

"His image has no relevance in the trial."

"Are you sure, sir? Have you ever heard of "collective unconscious" and "archetypes"? These are psychological structures built and perpetuated in the communities through symbolism. Churches have always controlled the tools that form consensus... through religious education, the pomp of worship and the placement of holy symbols in public places. Don't underestimate the Devil's image, sir, for he is fighting just for that."

Nick realized that the challenge was becoming increasingly complex.

∽∽∽

The days that followed saw the Swiss prosecution work assiduously to bring the various religions closer together and balance the East with the West, worlds that had always been distant from one another.

A Taoist master declared, "In nature, there are no substances that are one hundred per cent pure: in any element there is always a little of its opposite; therefore, there must be a little good in the Devil, just as there must be a little evil in God".

In a climate of moral and ideological tension, on the world's greatest stage, under the watchful eyes of the oriental leaders, Natalie Brinne listed the foul deeds committed by the demons in India after its fall. In the East, God was known as Brahma and the Trinity was completed by the figures of Shiva and Vishnu.

"The demon Kaitabha and his brother Madhu were able to steal the sacred Vedas texts," she denounced. "The demon Bali tried to attack the Empyrean, the highest heaven, but Vishnu punished him. And lastly Mahisha, the monstrous demon with the head of a buffalo, tried to break out and take the place of the divinity, but he was killed by the release of energy from all the forces in heaven."

Satan did not seem upset by the accusations. "Their ambition was to return to heaven, but they did not know how to do that. Frenzied and yearning for lost bliss; nobody should ever survive their own fall."

Somewhere else, a woman with red hair made her way through the onlookers in a bar at the Paradeplatz and reached the television screen from which the programme was being broadcast; all focus was on the screen and there were continuous comments.

Satan had never had any direct contact with the Chinese master Confucius or with the Taoist prophet Lao-Tze, but there had been intense clashes with Buddha.

The red-haired woman sat at a little table with her legs crossed, while the attorney continued the accusations, "With the name of Mara, the demon of death, you tried to corrupt Buddha, leading him away from the path of truth. You offered him all the powers and joys of life, didn't you?"

Bensoria the witch stifled a smile.

"I wanted to show the enlightened one that he was making a mistake," Lucifer replied, "and that renouncing bodily desires does not eliminate the suffering of the spirit."

Then he turned towards the television camera and, for a moment, it was as if he recognized Bensoria's face in the bar, through the screen. He stared at the screen and smiled.

The audience at home was bewildered by this.

Bensoria waved back to say hello to him from the bar. Only she could help the prince and she would soon be doing so.

13

The leaden cross

A weak afternoon sun shone on the white cloak of snow
that covered Zurich, painting the sparse clouds with
gold. In the law firm at the Weinplatz, a few men were intent
on formulating the defence for the next hearings, the theme
of which was going to be Christianity. Exhausted, Linda
rested in an armchair, while Frank was sprawled on the sofa,
surrounded by a sea of books, polishing his 38 calibre
revolver. The philosopher Von Hugh was at the window,
while the lawyer sat at his desk re-examining the sacred
writings. In that period, he was verifying the fact that the
sacredness of a text is inversely proportionate to its
intelligibility. Christ's two natures, "consubstantial" and that
of the "hypostatic union", had caused him considerable
confusion.

He closed the Gospel. "Sin, the end of the world, Hell…
how could it be called a "happy story"?"

Victor Von Hugh looked away from the window.
"Seeing an enemy burn can be a happy sight. The threat that
the Messiah loved to repeat to Hell, "there will be weeping

and gnashing of teeth", suggests quite a lot of satisfaction in imagining the scene".

But the lawyer did not seem convinced: "And what was the meaning of the parables?"

"The parables highlighted the value of authority," the other man explained. "God was depicted as a judge, a king, a master... The good shepherd recovers the lost sheep and takes it back to the fold as if it were an object. The father rewards the prodigal son when he returns home... In the parables, the human desire for freedom is not taken into consideration at all."

Nick still had some doubts. "I have noticed that Christ never smiled."

"It was probably the Devil who taught irony to man. Perhaps for him, being flippant was a way of flying again."

The lawyer flipped through the Gospels some more: "The Messiah made a fig tree wither because it had produced no fruit, when it was not the right season. In order to get rid of the demons who possessed a person, he made them enter into a herd of pigs and then made them fall off a cliff. His justice consisted of a search for scapegoats"

The other man did not answer and the lawyer continued, "Before Pontius Pilate, when interrogated about the meaning of the truth, Christ was silent... he said nothing".

"He had not had any difficulty preaching before the people," Von Hugh said, "but before a person like Pilate he remained silent. The question "what is the truth?" remained unanswered."

Nick got up and walked around the room, in front of the assistants, who were watching him in silence.

"In any case," he concluded, lingering in front of the book that lay there on the table, "we have enough material for the next hearings."

"He has nothing!" Bernard Louis blurted out, at the same time, in the prosecution's offices. "The lawyer is bluffing. He's a good poker player, but I know how to play too. The only thing we need more information on is the role of the Holy Spirit…," he said, raising his arms: "The way he descended upon the apostles is questionable: inspired by the breath of Jesus, according to *Gospel of St John*, or descended like tongues of fire, according to the *Acts of the Apostles*? We need more precise information."

"Shall I call the theological commission of Jerusalem?" Natalie asked.

"No, don't worry," he sighed. "I don't think that Valance will attack the Holy Spirit tomorrow."

"And what do you think he will attack?"

Louis stared at her, sure of himself: "The Messiah directly".

∽ ∽ ∽

In the main courtroom, next to the orthodox patriarch and the Protestant Evangelical pastor, Teomondo III was irritable as he loosened the collar of his cassock. Paradoxically, the spiritual unity that history had denied them was materializing now, thanks to the Devil's intervention: hatred, resentment and fear of the enemy were succeeding where brotherly love that was thousands of years old had failed.

The television cameras lit up the worried face of the judge, Tom Salomon, who was aware that the lawyer's line of defence had become an audacious attack on traditional values… and he was the unfortunate arbitrator.

Pacing with feigned perplexity, the lawyer resumed his examination of the accused, "Why did God choose Mary to give birth to the "Son of man", or the son of God, who was in fact God himself?"

Everyone present fell silent. The accused smiled. "He has always been attracted to virgins; young girls who have

145

not yet tasted the fruit of knowledge... Humble and without ambitions, Mary was perfect. "Here I am, I'm God's servant"," he said imitating a female voice to recreate the reply given by Mary to the angel Gabriel. "The Almighty thus poured forth his semen, the Holy Spirit, and fertilized her. But he refused to take responsibility and she was forced to ask Joseph for a remedial wedding. Joseph never suspected anything."

Bernard Louis ran his hand through his hair and Radio Maria, the Catholic broadcasting station, interrupted its live coverage.

"So the birth of Christianity depended upon a conception that went against nature?" Nick asked.

The Devil did not reply.

"And what was Christ's personality like?"

"He was torn apart by his double nature - human and divine. The son of God preached love for one's enemy, but as far as I, his greatest enemy, was concerned, he preached hatred. While teaching people not to judge, he dictated moral regulations. He promoted indulgence, but threatened the fires of hell upon those who did not listen to him. He proclaimed humility, but showed an excess of vanity and pride. He dreamed of equality among men, but established a priestly hierarchy. He invited people not to exchange any injustice, but defined the Pharisees a "race of vipers"... Although he urged people to express themselves in simple terms, with a "yes, yes or no, no", he used an obscure and metaphorical language and nobody understood the meaning of his parables. Even the gospels have been interpreted in multiple ways throughout history."

"In other words, his morality was aimed only at his neighbour, but not at himself. And why did the Father allow these contradictions?"

Satan did not reply right away and his eyebrows joined in a frown, as he concentrated. "Only by controlling extremes and handling contradictions can long-lasting power be preserved. With the crucifix, the symbol of the poor and the deprived, God was able to build an eternal kingdom."

The words echoed across the sea of engrossed faces, murmurs of temptations that never took form, and the discomfort felt by the Christians became tangible.

"And what about the miracles? Why did Jesus work miracles?"

"He resorted to miracles in order to make his doctrine more credible… The masses were always suspicious about his reasoning."

"But despite that, his contemporaries did not believe in him."

"He had overestimated people's gullibility."

"Objection," Bernard Louis intervened. "It was Satan who blinded men and led them not to recognize God in Jesus!"

Valance replied with a smile, "And since when have sons ever recognised their fathers? It is always up to fathers to recognize their sons!"

Some laughter was heard in the gallery and the judge reprimanded the lawyer.

The Devil's voice inflicted another blow, "Jesus healed a few cripples and blind people, but he didn't eliminate disease or poverty. He promised bliss in the afterlife in order to debase this world. He condemned prosperity and urged people not to work to hinder development. He induced people not to care about the future, to betray themselves, to put themselves last and to be poor of spirit, to prevent them from maturing and lead them back into the Eden of unawareness from which I had freed them!"

A loud buzz of objection arose in the audience.

"Two thousand years of Christian morals are being challenged!" Sophia remarked into the television microphones, "a topic that will create a debate between the experts."

A lawyer who, on the whole, seemed pleased with himself was pacing around the room.

"Tell us about the last supper. Why the ritual of the Eucharist?"

"An ancient *theophagy*, cannibalism established as a sacrament, a ritual conceived to induce men to share the master's destiny: sacrifice and death."

"But why was Jesus crucified? The people who had applauded his coming to Jerusalem on a donkey, condemned him when they chose Barabbas over him. Is it only possible to obtain consensus when on a donkey's back?"

The members of the audience in the room held their breath. The question of the death of Jesus was extremely important. Bernard avoided alluding to the responsibility of the Jews, for fear of stirring up new controversies.

"The people did not know what they were doing," the accused replied, "and therefore they were not responsible for the consequences." Lucifer half-closed his eyes: "Yahweh had prepared these events a long time before and he had drafted the script in the form of prophecies. The crucifixion of the Messiah served to purify sins and redeem the people. Christ was the scapegoat of humanity".

"What kind of justice would accept an innocent man as a scapegoat?" the lawyer asked. "The cross, the greatest symbol of human injustice, erected as a life model!"

The courtroom was as silent as a tomb, with so many questions destined to remain unanswered.

Somewhere outside, a rooster seemed to be crowing and an inexplicable sound of nails, wood and moaning filled the courtroom, creating anguish among those present, until the shadow of the Golgotha, the mountain of the Passion, appeared on the wall behind the jury. The prince of the underworld was a bridge of communication between present and past, between truth and illusion, and everyone had the impression that they were watching the Passion of Christ live.

However, it was just a momentary impression, as Nick then changed the subject. "And what about Judas? What role di Judas Iscariot have in all this?"

"Oh, Judas!" Satan exclaimed, in an affectionate tone of voice. "His crime was that of not believing in the master's divine nature, but his betrayal was necessary for the design to work: allowing the capture and crucifixion of Jesus. His weakness was exploited, the heavenly kingdom was built upon his sin, he was made into the scapegoat's scapegoat."

"You mean Judas is expiating in Hell to save us all?" Nick asked, guessing.

"Mr Valance!" the judge reprimanded him again.

"But there are two different versions of the death of Judas: one is suicide by hanging after having given back the thirty pieces of silver, while the other is a strange accident on a piece of land bought with those pieces of silver. Which is the real version?"

"You should ask the Holy Spirit," was his laconic reply.

"… Incompatible stories that lead us to suspect a simulated suicide, an artfully constructed crime. Basically, Judas was a witness that knew too much."

The insinuation stunned the Christian leaders, none of whom had ever considered this eventuality.

Aware of the growing attention, Valance continued, "Until, after his death on the cross and the defeat of man, God came out a winner! Or perhaps Jesus rose from the dead because he regretted having sacrificed himself? It's hard to say. And anyway, despite the redeeming event, the world continued to be full of sin".

"Yahweh believed that the tribulations of his son would encourage man's sense of guilt," Satan said, "but once again they continued to follow the path of progress."

While Satan spoke, Bernard Louis goaded the lawyer. "Surely you're not going to deny the resurrection of Christ now?"

"Come to think of it, his death was never verified by any doctor, and there was no declaration of presumed resurrection," Nick observed.

At that, the public prosecutor approached the defence's bench. "You're making a mistake by attacking Christ, Valance, and public opinion will not forgive you for it. This irony might cost you dearly".

But the devil's eyes flashed over the audience. "God inspired the Old Testament, he inspired the gospels, the Koran, the Vedas, the Bhagavad Gita, the Book of Mormon, various sacred works and dogmas and rituals that vary from religion to religion… because he knew that by spreading contrasting universal truths, men would hate and fight against each other, and that would slow down their growth!"

The judge rang his bell. "We will take a short break," he said, gasping for air.

A crucifix hanging on the wall suddenly came off and fell crashing to the ground.

∽ ∽ ∽

That same day, in Rome, the preacher, Joe Pelton, climbed up the Colosseum in order to hold another of his mystical sermons before an audience of delirious millenarians. "Christ ordered us to love our enemy and our enemy is the Devil! Therefore it is a sin to fight against evil: we must love Satan, help him and turn the other cheek!"

But the Italian police stopped him for instigating people to commit crimes.

At the same moment, the President of the United States entered the committee room at the Zurich town hall, where other politicians were awaiting him.

"He's a subversive !" he ranted. "He's seditious, a social threat!"

President Jershon was a man with a wrinkled face, like an old Texan, and had a swift way of doing things. Not having accepted the UN resolution on the trial taking place in Switzerland, he had stayed in Washington to follow the event on TV, but the recent developments had made it necessary for him to be present on-site.

«An arsonist who came up to bring fire to the valleys," Chancellor König confirmed.

"Why is it that nobody has been able to shut him up?" Jershon added. "Are we not perhaps in the cradle of western civilization?" he said with veiled irony.

President Renard replied with a diplomatic smile, "First of all, allow me to welcome you to the cradle of western civilization. Secondly, let me point out that western civilization itself is producing the accused's arguments. The Devil is a child of this civilization and he is turning against it. However, we are sure that good sense will prevail in the end".

"Let's hope that it won't be too late!"

Elsewhere, in the meeting room of an editorial office, the seemingly irritated director, along with several associates, read the draft of Sophia Madlane's last article.

"We are going too far, my girl. Nobody is asking you to pretend to be a theologian. The Devil's declarations are sufficient to bring in an audience without having to interpret them."

Sophia looked around, seeking the support of her colleagues. "But don't you understand? Jesus was used by God as an alibi, as a justification for the evil that exists in the world. If even the son of God suffers, then we must all suffer and, therefore, suffering is inevitable!"

The director, looking doubtful, rocked his head from side to side, and the others remained in silence.

"God has sacrificed his son to remain inert before human suffering: he put his son on the cross once so that it would remain on our shoulders forever!"

"This interpretation is extreme."

"Man addresses God especially when he's suffering: that's why God has made suffering divine!"

"It's better to be cautious, Sophia," he said, handing the article back to the woman. "Our headlines are being criticized enough for their "pro-diabolic" positions, of which you are the main representative. You are compromising yourself; it would be better to get someone else to do the reports".

The journalist got up, irritated. "You know very well that I am only seeking the truth… and the truth is locked inside cell 666!"

"Then go and look for it down there," the director said, provoking her.

Sophia left the room, slamming the door behind her.

The next day in the judge's office, Nick Valance made an application to summon God. He had enough material to try such a step.

"I think that there is a *fumus persecutionis* from Heaven against my client. Therefore, I ask that God and the Devil be made to confront each other in order to ascertain the truth. Furthermore, my client wishes to file a formal complaint against the Almighty for slander to his detriment and ideological perjury in sacred acts, as well as for abuse of omnipotence."

"That's ridiculous, your honour," Louis burst out, "it's just the umpteenth farce! The lawyer should be more respectful."

"The request is valid in formal terms…," Salomon said, hesitating and wiping the sweat from his brow, "but Heaven is effectively outside our jurisdiction."

After some insistence based on the law, for the first time in history the name of Yahweh was entered into the register of suspects, thus becoming subject to human justice. The atheists were amused and the masons rejoiced: finally Heaven was being challenged.

The consequences of such an event were unpredictable.

14

Desert wind

The Lord says: "Who will summon me?"

Jeremiah 49:19

While the prosecution was forced to launch a formal investigation into God, Victor Von Hugh drilled the lawyer about the foundations of Muslim theology, the subject of the next hearings. Acting as an intermediary between the Devil's word and the philosopher's interpretation, Nick went to the prison regularly and the picture that emerged comforted him regarding the line of defence he had adopted.

The midday sun was burning down on the city's tarmac streets and purple clouds, like scars in the sky, floated above the buildings. It was the first sunny day in a long time and, thanks to the Islamic religion, the public prosecution was overturning what had been said in the previous hearings. Before the proud gaze of the imam, Natalie Brinne accused Lucifer of having interfered with Mohammed's designs.

"The *jinns*, demons of the desert, tried to suffocate the prophet of Allah while he was sleeping. Do you confirm that?"

"It was a failure," Lucifer, replied looking worn out, "but Mohammed was introducing the concept of the "Holy war", the *jihad*, as a tool of political expansion."

Outside the building, several figures dressed in dark clothes were silently climbing down from the roof. Their shadows ran along the walls of the building like spiders on a web; on their heads, they wore turbans bearing the symbol of a crescent moon.

Natalie pressed the speaker, "However Mohammed succeeded in converting numerous demons by reading the pages of the Koran".

"They were lesser demons and certainly not much of a conquest for him."

The group stopped next to a large window. As soon as the wavering images on the mirror were in place, the leader spurred them on, "Only those who die in the holy war can enter the Garden of Delight, where pious and beautiful young girls await them".

Gripping the curved daggers between their teeth, the men loaded the machine guns and began to sway back and forth. The extremists had refused to represent themselves in the trial, since they considered it a ploy used by the Western world to monopolize the concept of evil, but the hearing under way had made a purifying action necessary.

While Natalie and Lucifer engaged in a duel, the maniple opened fire on the windows: "*Allahu akbar*, Allah is great!"

A shower of glass accompanied their entrance into the building. The people present jumped: a Brahman suffered an injury to his leg, a Buddhist monk suffered a wound to his arm, two Hare Krishnas in their colourful robes put down the toilet paper, timidly raising their hands. The terrorists realized that they were not in the main courtroom, but in one of the bathrooms in the Palace of Justice.

Embarrassed, they excused themselves and went back outside.

Not long afterwards, when Natalie Brinne was concluding her interrogation, one of the side windows was smashed and the group of men, like avenging angels, burst into the courtroom. The television cameras frantically filmed the scene: the people present screamed in panic and some of them threw themselves to the floor, while others tried to escape and a few began to invoke Allah.

The live images shocked the spectators.

"It's the end of the world!" the director blurted out excitedly.

Shooting rounds of bullets into the air, the terrorists moved towards the cell where the accused sat waiting for them, unperturbed.

"In the name of Allah," the leader recited, "we condemn you to death for the countless sins you have committed. The sentence will be carried out immediately".

"Would you kill an unarmed opponent?"

"The serpent must be crushed."

"Every warrior has the right to die with a weapon in his hand."

The leader hesitated, with his finger on the trigger; the great desert whisperer was now powerless before him and the glory of heaven inches away. Then he decided: "Let him out".

"But *Rais*…," the others cried.

"Do as I say!"

"He is brainwashing you…"

Yorgo Mirakis timidly came out from beneath a bench and approached the clerk of the court's table, where he picked up a bronze pitchfork, one of the artefacts found in the devil's hideout.

"Give him this," he suggested.

The terrorists looked at it, undecided.

"It is his weapon," the leader concluded.

The cell was opened and the infernal pitchfork was given to Satan: a weapon thousands of years old, forged in the underworld by Vulcan, the best demonic blacksmith.

"You will not be able to stop the silver bullets from my machine gun!"

Satan smiled, masking his aggressiveness with a sardonic expression, and began to rotate the weapon, making it spin faster and faster, until the points became incandescent.

At that moment, the door flew open and the UN's Blue Helmets burst into the courtroom. The terrorists did not hesitate to open fire, creating a ferocious shootout. In the general confusion, with the tear gas exploding between the benches, the commander took out his scimitar and hurled it at Satan intending to run it through him. He dodged the blow and grabbed the blade, making it retract: the blade had become cold like ice in his hands.

Then the east wind, the *khamsin*, the irresistible desert wind that, without any prior warning, rises to devour all it encounters in its path, made its way into the building and began to blow along the corridors, creating even greater confusion for everyone present. Judge Salomon hid on the floor, succumbing to the umpteenth heart attack, before a cloud of sand covered the bench.

Satan gave fleeting glances around the room: the wind was confusing the soldiers, the people were milling around the exits; it was a scene from hell.

He jumped on the tables, grabbed hold of the chandelier, projecting fragmented shadows on the walls, and then leapt towards the exit.

∽ ∽ ∽

In the corridors of the courthouse, pandemonium reigned supreme. Armed policemen ran towards the courtroom along with journalists and onlookers, while a great many people tried with all their might to get away. Satan proceeded cautiously through the sea of humans, swimming like a salmon against the tide. He succeeded in getting part of the way down the corridor but before he could reach the lifts, the exorcist, father Cimor, noticed him. His long hair and feline movements were unmistakable.

He appeared before him, armed with a crucifix: "Where do you think you're going, demon? You can trick the world, but you can't trick me!"

The Devil replied by blowing at the crucifix and setting it on fire.

The object fell to the floor and the devil grabbed his old rival by the throat.

"I'm unarmed...," Cimor gasped.

"You have your faith don't you?"

It was only then that the people present recognized him: "It's the Devil! He has escaped!"

A noisy crowd surrounded the two like a concentric wave and a compulsive flurry of flashes from cameras lit them up.

The Blue Helmets approached cautiously. "Alright, pal, stay calm... nothing has happened; let him go".

Lucifer's eyes frantically looked for a way out: at the end of the corridor, there were the lifts to the floor below. Abandoning Cimor, the demon opened his arms: his suit tore across theback and his bat wings appeared, as the bystanders screamed.

He started to run, making the terrified public move aside. Several policemen tried to block his way, but his shadow pushed them away. His open wings brushed against pictures of jurists in the room, creating an icy wind all around and then his body rose up. The demonic figure took flight along the corridors of the courthouse, like a bird of the night.

A great many people threw themselves to the ground while the depraved being flew over their heads.

Pope Teomondo, who was getting into the lift with the Swiss guards, caught sight of the huge bat heading towards him and pressed the button. The demon reached him as the doors were closing. He grabbed at the doors with his claws, but was unable to stop them and they locked with a thud, as Teomondo groaned with relief. The Devil would not have been the ideal guest at his lunch.

After looking around, the fugitive continued towards the steps that led to the floor below. At the top of the steps, a burst of machine gun fire grazed his back, perforating one of his wings. He fell, stifling the pain, and pulled his wounded limb back in; then he bounced onto the handrail of the steps and slid down it. A crowd was waiting at a safe distance in the room below.

Lucifer headed towards the exit as the photographers' cameras flashed, capturing him in motion.

A few metres from the main entrance door, just a few steps away from the world, a marksman was able to take aim.

He pressed the trigger lightly and a bullet sped towards Lucifer, who held back a scream as the bullet penetrated his back. He swayed, confused, as his body became heavy and his muscles went stiff. Everyone in the place seemed to be holding their breath.

He continued to walk towards the reddish light of dusk beyond the door, but he was unable to cross it.

He collapsed to the floor wheezing.

∽ ∽ ∽

The dramatic news echoed through the media, bouncing around every corner of the globe:

TERRORISTS BURST INTO THE COURTHOUSE,
DEVIL TRIES TO ESCAPE, BUT IS STOPPED.

While the world was in turmoil and the multinationals feared that the trial would be cancelled, Satan underwent surgery.

The bullet that had hit him had been shot from a tranquilizer gun, but it had caused internal lesions. The doctors took advantage of the moment to carry out a check-up and analyse his physical structure, observing that the being had no heart and, instead of blood, he had an acidic substance.

Later on, when Valance was able to see his client, he did not hide his disappointment. "Why did you try to escape" he reproached. "Your attempt to escape demonstrates guilt. If you don't trust my approach, I will withdraw from your defence."

Satan was chained to a small bed in the infirmary, guarded by numerous policemen and with drips in his arms. He was pale and tired, but satisfied for having survived the doctors.

"Don't ask for any acts of faith from me," he replied.

"Our theory risks being undermined by your behaviour."

"I'm not a sacrificial lamb and I cannot perish inside a cage." He stared at the ceiling. "If I vanish nobody will ever be able to oppose God again. Yahweh will have total control of the universe and his power will be absolute and unconditional".

With her white coat flapping, an old nurse came over to reproach the lawyer, "The patient needs to rest". She took the thermometer from the patient's armpit and checked it: "Zero degrees... well at least he hasn't got a fever".

The lawyer said goodbye with a wave, but before he could leave the room Satan called him back. "Mr Valance, I realize I made a mistake. Perhaps you're right. Maybe it's best to resign myself and succumb to this trial".

"Human justice is not perfect," Nick said, reassuring him, "you need not despair."

ⵯ ⵯ ⵯ

That same evening the politicians listened to the umpteenth television interview with the expert witness for the defence Von Hugh.

"Fundamentalism is a fall-back of religions onto themselves, a violent exclusion from the rest of the world, the proof of the crisis of a religion on a social level and of its inability to convince others…"

With a beard and turban, the Islamic imam turned off the television, shrugging. "We're sorry about what happened".

The American president banged the table with his fist. "Terrorists have been tormenting us for decades with attacks and hijackings and now that they could have done something useful, they failed. They missed their only chance to redeem themselves!"

"I would not advise you to attack the Devil again, gentlemen," President Renard said. "It is never wise to make your enemy into a martyr, as you would risk transforming him into an immortal symbol. Don't forget what happened to Jesus Christ."

"But what shall we do?" the German chancellor exclaimed. "Just helplessly sit here and watch this tragedy?"

The French president tried to relativize, but he wasn't convincing: the ancient serpent had slipped through their fingers.

In Hell, the news of the attack had caused unpredictable repercussions. Dissident fringe groups had tried to centralize power and numerous souls had escaped from the circles of Hell.

In the snowy countryside of Uetilberg, to the south of Zurich, in a gypsy campsite, Bensoria the witch had contacted the devil Astaroth through her crystal ball.

"I carried out an inspection in the city," she said "and I got close to the courthouse, but it's too protected for me to enter. I need to find a route to the prison. Time is running short, I fear…"

In the crystal ball, the bearded face of Astaroth, the demon of rationality, fidgeted in a cloud of smoke; the coverage wasn't the best this time.

"They want to shut Satan up before sentencing," he accused. "At this point, they fear his testimony. But we will know how to answer: we have sent you a few documents that should sort things out."

"Documents? And what am I supposed to do with them?"

"You will need to deliver them to a person in Zurich, who will know how to make the best use of them."

Astaroth's face disappeared into the cloud of smoke, leaving Bensoria worried. Astaroth was a great strategist, but this battle against Heaven was out of their league.

The witch recited a magical spell and connected via a satellite channel, on which a journalist was commenting on the attack that had taken place and the results of the analyses to which the Devil had been subjected.

She picked up the popcorn and sat on a table with her legs crossed.

A few hours later, when the inhabitants of the gypsy campsite were resting and a gentle breeze from the east embraced the white edges of the countryside, she was roused by the flapping of wings at the window of the shack. Bensoria went to open it to let the big black bird in.

"Hello Puck," she said, pleased to see him and letting him sit on her arm, "you got here quickly."

The crow cawed. There was a roll of black leather attached to his claw.

15

The witch's touch

Exodus 22:18

When the main entrance door opened and light footsteps climbed the stairs towards the top floor, it was almost a quarter to midnight and the lights were still on in Nick Valance's studio. A silent presence entered, sneaking into the apartment without any difficulty, and knocked gently on the studio door.

Nick was not expecting any visits and, through the clouded glass, he could make out the shape of a female form.

"Come in," he called.

A gust of wind blew in as the door opened and a middle-aged woman wearing a dark dress came into the room. Nick looked puzzled as her long red hair moved by itself to close the door; it was not the type of client he usually dealt with.

"Can I help you?" he asked.

The woman's answer was ambiguous. "I'm here to see you, Mr Valance. I need to talk to you about case 666 and your client".

"You should come back during office hours," Valance pointed out, having already received numerous visits from tricksters and lunatics.

With a theatrical gesture, the woman showed him a black leather folder. "I have something that might help you".

She put it on the table, before Nick, feeling annoyed, could get up and she opened it and took out a few strange documents that had become yellowed with the passing of time.

The lawyer warily leaned forward to look at them. "What are they?" he asked, taking them and giving them a quick glance, just as the light from the table lamp revealed their content to him. "They look like deeds of... ," He didn't finish the sentence, as an interested expression appeared on his face. "But... are they authentic?"

"You decide," Bensoria replied, her deep black eyes twinkling.

"How did you get them?"

"I'm sure that you will be able to use them in the best possible way."

"But who are you?"

"My name is not important. I just needed to deliver them to you."

Valance examined them more carefully in the lamplight. "Who would have thought it?" he said, turning to the woman: "Listen...," But the woman had disappeared. The room was empty.

Astonished, he looked around and went out into the corridor: there was no one there. The woman had vanished. She had faded away like a dream at dawn. The lawyer rubbed the back of his neck and returned to his desk to stare at documents. They were undoubtedly in his hands.

"Jackpot," he murmured.

On the ledge of the half-closed window, a black cat watched in silence.

∽∽∽

In the Rathaus building, the political leaders had met for high-level talks, when the English prime minister, Lady Fillingham, walked in, with a dark look on her face, and took a seat at the table. She was holding a file on which the words TOP SECRET were written.

"We have had the umpteenth confirmation from our detectives," she reported. "Nothing! His past is crystal clear."

"Everyone has a skeleton in the closet," the American president insisted.

"He has always led a quiet life: just home and court." She opened the file: "Nick Valance lives with his wife in a little house in Abbey Road, a residential area of London; his studio is in Queen Victoria Street. They haven't got any children, just a dachshund. They are creatures of habit and they don't frequent high society. She is a member of a cookery club, he has no lovers, does not support any political parties and has never had any tax problems. We have bugged the telephones, but nothing compromising has been revealed".

"*Mein Gott!* We must continue, something will come out in the end!" the German chancellor exclaimed.

"We are looking at not one but two monsters," the American president ruled.

"Let's not exaggerate…," Renard suggested, but he was interrupted when the secretary suddenly came in, announcing, "Ladies and gentleman, the lawyer Nick Valance is asking to meet with you".

The politicians said nothing. Nobody was expecting a similar visit. Lady Fillingham hid the file.

"I wonder what he wants?" König said, looking concerned.

"Lawyers never come to announce good news," the Russian president predicted.

After a short discussion, Nick Valance was asked to come in and the heads of state welcomed him. They asked him to sit down and offered him something to drink, but he declined. They all scrutinized him, knowing that he was more diabolic than the client he was defending. After a few quick pleasantries, Nick illustrated the reason for his visit: he pulled a few documents out of his briefcase and, coming straight to the point, handed them to the people present.

The politicians felt an icy shudder run down their spines.

The lawyer leaned back in his chair and watched them turn pale. "Of course, they are just photocopies. The originals are in a safe place, but I think that each one of you will recognize your own signature in blood, at the bottom, followed by the letters *Stn*... Satan's initials."

The Russian president suddenly felt ill, the American stopped chewing his gum and chancellor König collapsed to the floor.

"How did you get these?" the French president asked, maintaining his self-control.

"I don't think it's important how I got them."

"They date back to many years ago...," someone admitted, "I was young and ambitious."

"They are still valid," Valance continued. "You sold your souls to the Devil in exchange for political power. These contracts are not subject to withdrawal and have no expiry date."

A wave of silence flooded the room. The male politicians loosened their ties, remembering that night, so many years before, on which they made a pact with the devil. Icy fingers caressed their napes and for a moment their shadows seemed to disappear.

"My client kept his part of the bargain, allowing you to obtain top leadership in your states, but you did not live up to the commitment negotiated, plotting behind his back to falsify the trial." He paused for a moment and then carried on, "If Satan were to die, these contracts would become ineffective and your souls would be saved. But a contractual commitment is sacrosanct. By revealing the conflict of interest that you have with this trial, I could have the entire procedure cancelled".

"No, not that…," the heads of state exclaimed. "Public opinion would never forgive us if that were to happen."

Hiding his satisfaction, Nick reflected: "It is fair that the trial be carried out in respect of the rules, but there will be no more attacks, nor blackmail. If something should happen to my client, the originals of these documents will be sent to the prosecutor's office and to the press".

The politicians nodded wanly.

"But do you realize what you are doing?" President Jershon blurted out. "In this way , you will let the world fall into chaos... into anarchy!"

The lawyer smiled. "But perhaps I will win the case." he said as he got up and, before leaving, added, "While I was reading these contracts, I asked myself: is a politician's soul really worth so much?"

He shook his head and disappeared.

∽ ∽ ∽

Across the icy surface of the lake, a big black cat reached the port of Horgen, on its way to the imposing maximum security prison. The fog wrapped itself around the Bezirksgebäude building, where armed soldiers moved along the watchtowers, like tormented souls in Purgatory. Feeling an imminent threat, the dogs whimpered nervously, forcing the guards to walk around and check several times; but the feline was able to enter the prison without being seen. The cat moved silently, following its sense of smell: the ventilation grille on the wall was not high and the cat reached it with one jump.

Locked inside his underground cell, Lucifer could not see the moon trembling faintly through a thick layer of mist, but he could feel it; the energy of the moon reached him, regenerating him. His skin had become white and his lips were ashen. He ran his hand through his ruffled hair, uncovering his dark eyes.

He had tried to look at himself in the mirror, but in vain: his image could not be reflected. The lord of the night sat irritated on the edge of the bed. He had been unable to see his face for thousands of years and he had forgotten what he looked like. God had created the angels so that he could see the reflection of his own perfection in them. They had been his personal mirrors; but when Lucifer rebelled, he lost his power to reflect light. He could only absorb it and, in this way, he had become invisible in any mirror. Mirrors, after all, reflect the truth and he represented lies.

He let out a little groan of pain and the mirror in front of him shattered into a thousand pieces, as sharp splinters covered the floor like sparkling tears. He sat there in silence, listening to the faint voice of the moon. The moon spoke to him every night, telling him what was going on in the world, and that night a guest was coming to see him. Lucifer could smell the guest.

Suddenly, there was a scratching on the ventilation grill of his cell. The Devil went over to it and heard some mewing coming from the narrow duct. Only a cat could get through it. He yanked the grill open, widening the bars and creating a little passageway, until he could see the outline of the animal with its sparkling eyes. The cat leapt out into the room, greeting him with a meow; the black cat had a red tuft on its head and, as Lucifer watched, it lifted itself up onto its hind legs and underwent a mutation: its body grew larger and its fur began to disappear, uncovering white human skin. The prince smiled, admiring the naked body taking shape before him.

"Nice to see you again, Bensoria, after all this time."

She stretched her limbs. "I have always suffered from claustrophobia, but I'm happy to have found you, my lord." He went over to her and hugged her affectionately. The witch's long red hair waved sensually, like tentacles, caressing the back of the prisoner's neck. "We don't have much time on our hands. I have sabotaged the closed circuit cameras: they can't see us, but they will soon come to check."

"It hurts me not to be able to offer you anything," he said.

"How can you joke? Your life is at stake here."

"My life? I have always lived other people's lives, Bensoria, nourishing myself from their emotions; I have never known what it means to live."

Bensoria gently touched his face. It was Lucifer who had helped her start practicing black magic some centuries before. He had seduced her and transmitted his knowledge to her and she had become a witch because of her love for him.

"We are all fallen angels, my lord," she said, "but you have a more important purpose: the destiny of the world depends on your existence. The Underworld Council wants to organize a command unit to free you: they are digging an underground tunnel to your cell. The legions of demons are ready to intervene."

Satan frowned, turning his back on his guest: "I do not want to escape, I have decided to succumb to this judgment".

"What?" she exclaimed in disbelief. "Why should you do that?"

He shrugged. "I have decided."

"But you will be executed!"

"I must trust human law. After all, I spent thousands of years inspiring it."

"Do you think God would allow anything to go against his will?"

"With a little bit of optimism."

"But this is madness, my Lord."

The Devil went over to her and took her face in his hands. "I'm tired of running, Bensoria. I'm tired of being persecuted, of being the scapegoat for everything that doesn't work in the world. The trial may be a solution: whether they convict me or acquit me, evil will disappear. And a buried devil will be more useful to our ideal than a fugitive devil".

"Is there nothing I can do to make you change your mind?"

He said no, shaking his head.

"Hell will never accept this."

"There is something you can do, though." A strange light danced in his eyes, like a flash on the dark horizon of his thoughts. "This is the reason why I wanted to talk to you. Satia is here... I saw her... and I need to meet her."

"Satia... *your* Satia?"

"She has finally been reincarnated: I have sent her a few oneiric messages and she has tried to come to me, but so far they have not allowed her to. Perhaps you can help me."

The witch seemed surprised, "Satia, that's incredible... Well, I'll think something up".

Lucifer clenched his fist. "This is not how I wanted to see her! Not in this circumstance. This too is a twist of fate"

Bensoria hugged and kissed him. His lips were cold and dry. Then she left. She knelt down and in a puff of smoke her body got smaller, dark fur began to cover her skin and the form of a cat replaced her human appearance. With an agile leap, she went back into the ventilation duct and, with a meow, she let herself be swallowed up by the darkness. Satan carefully closed the grill and curled up again in a corner of his cell, overwhelmed by a sea of memories.

"Satia…"

16

In the footsteps of Providence

> For who will say, "What hast thou done?" Or will resist thy judgment? Who will accuse thee for the destruction of nations which thou didst make? Or who will come before thee to plead as an advocate for unrighteous men? For neither is there any god besides thee... to whom thou shouldst prove that thou hast not judged unjustly;

Wisdom 12:12 et seq.

Swimming in an ocean of dense theology, Nick Valance spent the next few afternoons with his philosophy adviser, trying to clarify the most obscure points of religious history... all the sacred beams and motes were put through a fine sieve.

"Christ gave Peter the task of building the Church... but with what resources?"

"With charity from the poor," Victor Von Hugh replied. "The proselytes were found among the less wealthy classes."

"So, the Church had to build altars and temples, maintain the clergy and spread the religion with the poor people's money?"

The adviser picked up the Scriptures and read from the Epistles of Paul, "One who is taught the word must share all good things with the one who teaches"; "Do we not have the right to eat and drink? Or is it only Barnabas and I who have no right to refrain from working for a living?" And Moses also said something similar, "The priests' dues from the people: the first fruits of your grain, of your wine and of your oil, and the first fleece of your sheep, you shall give him".

"Does this mean that the Churches had their own interests at heart?"

The door opened before Von Hugh could reply and Frank Moroni entered the room, looking radiant. "Boss, I've got interesting news: Purgatory was not established until the Middle Ages!"

"Purgatory?"

"A contact of mine at the Vatican confided in me." The detective threw his cigarette butt onto the carpet, shaking a light sprinkling of snow off of his shoulders. "Purgatory is never mentioned in the Scriptures".

"It's true," Von Hugh confirmed. "The dogma dates back to the Council of Trent, in the sixteenth century."

"Perhaps God established it in order to compete with the Devil, who was taking too many souls away from him," Moroni suggested.

"However, the orthodox Churches and the Protestants never recognized it," the philosopher specified.

The lawyer was confused. "Why establish it so late?"

"Purgatory is a sort of prison," Von Hugh said, "where souls are forced to expiate their sins, until someone lets them out by paying their "bail"; in fact, suffrage masses can shorten the penalty."

Nick passed his hand through his hair: "So, it is not about the rehabilitation of the sinner? If all you have to do is pay, then the rich are at an advantage."

"In fact, Martin Luther's Protestant Reform emerged from the scandal about the indulgences. God's laws were written allegorically to allow each of his ministers a wide scope when interpreting them and to make himself indispensable on every occasion in human life: births, weddings, illnesses, death…"

"So there is no certainty regarding the penalty."

Nick walked across the room with his hands behind his back. Slowly, the outline of the path of religious history became increasingly clear and the image that was appearing was more negative than he had imagined.

"There are too many mysteries in religions; from faith to the covenant, from the Trinity to the visible and invisible society of the Church... And over the centuries, an investigation has never been launched and no light has been thrown on the situation."

Fragments of truth, like a mosaic in pieces, lay scattered around them. But perhaps it was possible to understand the great design; the serpent of doubt had hissed its truth.

Now alone, the lawyer was thinking about the press review of recent days. The press was a sound box that distorted the events taking place at the trial. Any spectacularization obscured and reduced the possibility of reasoning; unless the argument were also spectacular and unless you were to use this weapon to your advantage. As he looked out of the window, his image on the glass brought back a smile to his face. He searched through the papers on his desk until he found a journalist's request to interview the Devil.

He had ignored it up until now, but perhaps it was time to pay some attention to it.

∽∽∽

In front of an increasingly hostile and distrustful audience, Valance introduced the historical events that followed the death of Jesus, illustrating the dramatic episode of Ananias and Sapphira.

"Who were these two?" the judge murmured to the clerk of the court, who had never heard of them.

Nick continued, "According to the Scriptures, two young newlyweds, Ananias and Sapphira, wished to enter the Christian community. They sold their farm in order to lay the proceeds "at the apostles' feet". However, they had kept a part of the proceeds for themselves and, when St Peter found out, he reproached the man so severely that he dropped dead, due to a probable apoplectic stroke".

The audience in the room was surprised to hear this.

"His wife suffered a similar fate," the lawyer continued. "Without informing her of her husband's death, St Peter asked her how much they had sold the land for and, when he heard her confirm her husband's false version, he threatened her so harshly that she also died suddenly. "Behold, the feet of those who buried your husband are at the door, and they will carry you out." From that moment, a great fear spread through the Christian community," he concluded "and nobody dared refuse St Peter a loan again."

Bernard Louis got up to reply, "Ananias and Sapphira were miserly and they were liars. It was only right to inflict an exemplary punishment on them".

"Ananias and Sapphira were murdered for money, your honour," the lawyer specified.

"Even if they were, it is irrelevant in today's trial."

Valance insisted, "Nevertheless, even today the Churches continue to be financed by their followers, which raises legitimate doubts about the impartiality of their teaching.". He pulled out Paul's Epistles and read a few passages: ""I have received full payment, and more. I am well supplied, having received from Epaphroditus the gifts you sent, a fragrant offering, a sacrifice acceptable and pleasing to God. "; "...this service is not only supplying the needs of the saints...". But, why don't the saints get funding from God," he lashed out, "after all, they work for him".

The insinuation caused a wave of indignation, but the lawyer did not give up. "The God of the Jews used the Christian religion to cause the collapse of the Roman Empire… and in the fourth century, when Christianity came to power, instead of being persecuted, it became the persecutor: God saw to it that the Christians became divided among themselves and that the dogmas produced schisms, excommunications and anathemas, leaving a trail of blood behind them as they went".

The judge, by now resigned, emptied out his last box of pills.

"Through Judaism, Christianity and Islam, God spread the crime of heresy throughout the world. It was a crime of opinion that the previous cultures had ignored." He raised a finger sternly: "For over a thousand years, the Christian countries condemned free thinkers to be burned at the stake and, in the Muslim countries, they were subjected to lynching. They were lay martyrs, men who sacrificed their lives and souls for their ideal, and to whom even the hope of heaven was denied".

The audience jumped at the word "martyrs".

""If anyone does not abide in me he is thrown away like a branch and withers; and the branches are gathered, thrown into the fire, and burned", the word of Jesus."

"You are only showing the negative aspect, Mr Valance," the public prosecutor said. "The heretics of that period were subversives of the social order and their condemnation was inevitable."

Nick nodded: "Witches, psychopaths, madmen and demented visionaries… all victims unaware of the right of every man to believe in whatever he wants". Inexplicable smells of smoke and burning flesh were perceived in the air. "Who inspired religious fervour, the crusades, fanaticism? Who replaced the Roman adversarial trial with the inquisitorial canonical one that disregarded the rights of the defence? It was an earthly dictatorship, a prelude to the heavenly one."

"The errors of a Church cannot be attributed to God!" Bernard objected.

"Nevertheless the Holy Spirit was present and must have inspired those actions," Nick replied, "and being immaterial he cannot, like Pilate, wash his hands of it! Not to mention the infallibility of the Pope...," Nick said, pulling out other documents. "If forty schisms violated St Peter's cathedra, twenty-seven covered it with blood; the conflicts between the Empire and the priesthood lasted more than six centuries. The Holy Spirit allowed for two or three popes to be elected, who reigned simultaneously, excommunicating each other. There were popes who had dissolute lives, popes elected at the age of twenty or murdered in their lovers' beds; popes who bought and resold the papacy, popes who were the sons of other popes... Urban VI, Clement XII, Alexander VI, Sergius III, Felix V, John X, John XI... As we can see", he said sarcastically, "papal infallibility is the only dogma abundantly demonstrated by history."

Unrest was growing in the room and Louis hesitated, his forehead creased with deep wrinkles, then banging his fist on the table: "It was the Devil who corrupted the message of the Gospel! That's why Martin Luther intervened and reformed and corrected it". He pointed at the accused: "What can you tell us about the great reformer? Is it true that you savagely attacked him in Wartburg castle, in West Thuringia?"

The episode of the fight between Luther and the Devil was well-known to the protestants.

The Devil got up and gripped the bars with both hands. "There was a physical fight between Luther and I, one night. I scattered nuts on the ground and he threw an inkwell at me". The steel bars the devil was holding began to sizzle. "His intention to reform the Church was a threat."

Nick pulled out some more documents. «Copernicus, Galileo, Bruno, Darwin and Freud are just a few victims of divine obscurantism. When Franklin invented the lightning rod, the clergy condemned the invention as an attempt to hinder divine lightning! The Church also opposed the freedom of the press, with the encyclicals *Mirari vos*, *Libertas* and the famous *Syllabus of errors*."

"This is not a harangue, Mr Valance!" Salomon reprimanded him.

Leaning on his bench, Nick added, "But from the Enlightenment on, the Devil gained ground, spreading tolerance and human values. "Tolerance" is an unknown word in the Scriptures. If today's religions have become more civilized, it isn't God's merit, but it came about thanks to the teachings of generations of free-thinkers, men who were once persecuted by Heaven. It happened thanks to my client's influence!"

∽ ∽ ∽

In the meeting room at the Town Hall, the politicians were watching the maxi-screen; nobody was in a fit condition to comment on such a devastating hearing. From the moment the lawyer had incriminated them with those contracts, politics had been excluded from having any control over the trial and the string of events had become a noose, a trap and yet another evil twist that they could not avoid.

During the adjournment, Valance approached his client's cell to speak to him. "It's Louis's turn to interrogate you now. Don't underestimate him: after the initial moment of surprise, the prosecution is getting organized and will dig deep and do everything it can to make you contradict yourself".

The bell rang, announcing that the hearing was starting again, just like in a boxing match when everyone returns to

181

their own corners. Bernard Louis approached the accused. "Would you illustrate the organizational structure of Hell to us?"

A topic like this was unexpected and the Devil gave a look of surprise at the defence bench before answering: "In the Middle Ages, Hell was a small empire. Kings and dukes lead legions of demons, in conflict with each other, and reactionary fringe groups altered its instability. Once I was dethroned... but today an elected principality exists as well as a council of archons with advisory functions, a *demonocracy*, that has so far confirmed me as the leader".

The news aroused a great deal of amazement among theologians. Touching his jaw, Bernard Louis pondered over the next moves to make. With the consensus of Erik Marduk, he had decided to initiate the most serious accusation, a choice that not everyone would have shared.

"It appears that, in your Hell, you torment souls and you make them burn by subjecting them to the most atrocious inhuman suffering. Does this correspond to the truth?"

A hesitation was perceived, when the accused did not answer.

The religious leaders appeared confused. "Punishing sinners is not a sin. Otherwise what would be the point of Hell?"

Satan seemed annoyed as he unveiled another mystery. "After Yahweh confined us to the Underworld, he allowed us to go up to Earth and tempt humans, in order to put them to the test. He wanted to choose them, select them, using the work we did".

"Did you have God's permission to work in the world?"

God used us so that his law would be respected... and we accepted the challenge to show him that humanity was on our side. Through man, the eternal fight between the opposing forces that God and I had personified, the ancient duel that had marked the origin of the world, had come to

Earth. Relegating us to act as prison warders to the souls he damned, God entrusted us with the task of torturing and tormenting them. He did not want to soil his hands personally."

"Evil being subcontracted," Valance denounced.

As if evoked by the Devil, the sudden cries of damned souls emerged from the depths of Hell, hanging heavily over the room, cries of pain and torment, spasm and tribulation. The judge had yet another heart fibrillation.

"Hell, God's Holy Inquisition," the lawyer said thoughtfully.

"But now the agreement has been concluded," the accused said, stunning everyone again. "At the beginning, Yahweh let me get close to the Empyrean so that I could accuse men. Every damned soul was a defeat for God. But then he noticed that he had lost too many and, after Jesus Christ had been lifted up, he permanently banished me from heaven, making his son an intercessor of souls, a public defender… With the policy of forgiveness and the establishment of Purgatory, the number of saved souls began to increase and the relationship between Hell and Heaven became tense. So I realized that something else could be done, a hope could be conceived, a spiritual army could be created."

"A spiritual army?"

"To aim for the re-conquest of Heaven."

"What?" the people present exclaimed, aghast.

"Today the souls that fall into the Underworld are no longer oppressed, but prepared for the inevitable conflict. On Judgement Day, Armageddon, the place in which the powerful of the Earth will reunite, we unite together to face the Almighty."

In the control room, the producer was trembling with excitement. "Quick, zoom in on him!"

The Devil's sparkling eyes transfixed the auditorium. "Nobody knows the conclusion of the challenge. It will be man who holds the balance of power, the last judge of the truth. The destiny of the world, the boundaries between Heaven and Earth, the victory of good or evil.. everything will come from human choices".

The voices and thoughts in the room vanished into the silence and Lucifer's words, translated into various languages, continued to hover around the room. "Everything will derive from human choices…"

As soon as the judge closed the hearing, great confusion exploded on all sides. The millenarians around the courthouse indulged in acts of violence and disorder was reported everywhere.

In an interview, professor Von Hugh threw more fuel onto the fire. "Hell is immoral blackmail: it forces people into a form of demoralizing obedience and its eternity is disproportionate compared to any crime."

The lawyer, Mr Valance, was escorted to his car by the guards while the journalists bombarded him with questions and the television cameras tried to follow him.

A worshipper was able to make his way through the crowd and get to him before he was swallowed up by his car. "If what the Devil has said is true and if everything that has been said in this trial is true, what do I do now?" he yelled desperately. "How should I behave with God?"

"Find yourself a lawyer,0" Nick replied.

The preacher, Joe Pelton, was holding another of his mystical sermons on top of Big Ben in London, high up above an adoring crowd: "Religions have obscure and mysterious designs and obscurity is darkness! The true light, the true story, is that God's infinite kindness makes all moral rules and regulations useless. Sin does not exist, punishments do not exist, Hell does not exist!"

While a sudden, violent thunderstorm hit Zurich, Teomondo III returned to his hotel, feeling shaken. In his double room with a view at the Zurich Marriott Hotel, he looked for an object he had brought from Rome. He could not put it off any longer. Nobody knew what was happening.

He picked up a little golden chest from a shelf inside the wardrobe. It had always been on his mind. He opened it with the key hanging from his belt and took out a few letters: three epistles with the words "Third prophecy" written on one of them in a woman's handwriting.

Breathing deeply, he unfolded it and examined what he had only once before had the courage to do during his papacy. Nobody else had ever been able to do it.

On the paper, which had yellowed over time, were the following words, written in Portuguese: "Revelation received on 13 October of the year of our Lord 1917". It was a document a couple of pages long, at the bottom of which was the signature of Lucia Dos Santos.

Teomondo covered his face. He knew that behind this name was the unmistakable signature of the mother of Jesus, Our Lady of Fátima.

Ever since the last survivor of the three shepherds of Fátima who had seen the Virgin Mary, had transcribed the revelations received, the precious documents had been jealously guarded by the Vatican.

The first two prophecies about the Russian Revolution and the fall of Communism had come true, but the third, the famous "Secret of Fátima", had been the object of conjecture all over the world for a long time.

The Pope who had received it, Pius XI, disturbed by its content, had decreed that it must remain sealed and his successors had ordered the same. Various rumours were circulating on the subject of the effects suffered by those who had read it. A pope had been found dead in his bed, after just 33 days of his papacy, with the letter in his hand. Another had been injured in an attack in St Peter's square on the anniversary of the first Marian apparition, after having decided to disclose its content. The Vatican had then authorized the publication of several extracts, confirming the theory of its fulfilment, but the full text had never been published.

Aware of that, Teomondo plucked up courage before beginning to read the complete text:

> *I write in obedience to the Holy Virgin so that she will light up the world and protect the bishop dressed in white when, injured, he crosses the city in ruins...* (indecipherable words) *The whole of humanity must correct itself and ask for forgiveness for its sins, because a great trial awaits it...* (deleted words) *In the last days, the last days of the Devil, the creature of evil, Satan, will come to Earth and will be captured by men. Human justice will be able to judge him and punish him for his foul crimes, preparing the advent of the kingdom of the Lord. But the ancient serpent is very astute and slippery... When fire and sulphur from the sky...* (illegible text)

The last words were impossible to understand and the text ended abruptly, as if someone had torn it.

Teomondo shut his eyes tightly to curb his emotion. The Virgin Mary's proclamation had come true, fully and irrefutably. He, Teomondo III, was the only one in the whole world that knew. He had been tempted, ever since the trial had begun, to share this information with humanity. The Church would have benefitted from it in terms of image, but he had preferred to play for time... and now he was beginning to feel afraid.

He looked at the ambiguous ending again, with its cryptic tone: "the ancient serpent is very astute and very slippery... "

17

Angel's ashes

Love covers all offenses

Proverbs 10:12

That evening, Sophia Madlane could hardly believe it when she finally got access to the maximum security prison of Horgen. Someone cautiously opened the steel reinforced doors for her, leading to the underground levels, accompanying her through the depths of obscurity, along a path dotted with sophisticated security systems. The journalist had wanted to be taken before the Devil, to interview him and do what nobody had ever dared to do before. The truth was locked inside that cell and she was going to find it. She had appealed to all of her acquaintances to get there and, in the end, she had obtained permission to enter the prison-bunker of Bezirksgebäude. The permission unexpectedly granted by the lawyer, Valance, had also been crucial.

At the end of a wide corridor, the Devil's cell awaited her, with its usual smell of sulphur.

Welcomed by the sound of Beethoven's *Fifth symphony* broadcast by cable radio, Sophia cautiously walked up to cell 666, a dark cell protected by a pane of glass, that the prisoner had recently personalized by decorating the walls with symbols and incomprehensible words, written in blood.

Sophia admired it. The layout of the room seemed unnatural: the bed was tilted on one side, the table and chairs seemed to have been dumped on the wall, a neon light was hanging diagonally and a few objects were floating in the air. It looked like a place from another world, a fragment of another dimension. Scientists had been secretly studying this unique phenomenon for weeks: the magnetic fields provoked by the demon altered the laws of physics, but the news had been kept top secret.

At last she saw him.

Lucifer was standing on one side of the room, smiling as if he had been expecting her. Sophia noticed that his silhouette cast no shadow on the floor.

"*Imperador del Doloroso Regno* (Emperor of the Kingdom of Despair)," she said, quoting Dante and trying to stay calm. "Please excuse me if I'm disturbing you at this hour."

"No hour would be better than this," the prisoner assured her, while a clock in the corridor struck twelve.

Around them, time seemed to flow irregularly.

"My name is Sophia Madlane and I'm a *New York Times* correspondent. I would like to interview you."

"I know who you are," he said, "I was expecting you."

"Will you grant me an interview?"

"I do not normally appreciate journalists. Too many public opinions crowd private ones… But you will be a pleasant exception."

Satan came close to the glass and looked at the woman, with her dark brown hair, light eyes and determined expression. She was a woman willing to do anything to get to the truth: even risk her soul.

"I fear that one night will not be sufficient," he said. "I have so much to tell, if mankind wants to listen to me."

"Let's try," she said with a smile, taking out a small video camera.

The prisoner's voice had a warm ring to it. "I have seen God's thunderbolts rip through the sky, I have felt the chasms of the earth open up, I have listened to the crying and grinding of teeth of thousands of souls, yet I never cease to be amazed by a woman's smile".

Sophia was impressed. "Are you always such a gentleman?"

"Never," he replied.

She bowed her head to conceal her blushing and began to seek some questions. He looked at her, digging deep into her soul, penetrating her thoughts and the things hiding behind her thoughts.

"I noticed that your body does not cast a shadow," the woman said.

"I am growing weak. The light passes through me without hitting me. After all, I am already a shadow... the shadow of a soul lost in the light of an impossible dream."

She cleared her throat. "A lot has been said about you in literature. How much of what has been attributed to you is true?"

He shrugged. "A great many artists have written about me, thinking they know me... Milton, Goethe... But they were only transfiguring their own fantasies. Tempter, flatterer, torturer, creator of sins, master of immorality; I am just a mask, a loose cannon.".

"And why have you always been considered so evil?" she asked.

"Because evil has always been seen as a state of chaos, indiscrimination and opposition to order... and who, more than I, is a symbol of opposition?"

"But don't you think that disorder is bad?"

"Disorder is order that cannot be understood."

"And what is evil?"

Lucifer put the palm of his hand against the glass. "Evil is need," he whispered, "as it constitutes a limit. You need what you don't possess. The further away you are from perfection, the more you need God. I have broken the fences, broken the banks, scattered the good shepherd's sheep. But, once upon a time, I taught the sheep not to need a shepherd anymore. I have pushed men to be rich in spirit and independent and, every time a man learns to think freely, breaking the chains of mental slavery, he is taking a step forward on the path to progress."

A shiver ran down the woman's spine. "Is this the difference between your morality and God's?"

"The Almighty has taken advantage of your weaknesses. He transformed fear into duty and resignation into virtue. He enhanced the value of humility because the humble make him feel big; he spread compassion in order to increase the depressing effect of suffering, he glorified faith and gullibility because scepticism and rationality can unmask him. He wanted to be known through love because it is the sentiment that obscures critical thinking more than any other... and lastly, he prohibited judgement... for fear of being judged." Lucifer declared, "Which morality needs to be sustained by the promise of heaven or by the threat of hell?"

"And what about your own morality?" the woman provoked.

"I adore freedom, courage, intelligence, beauty, the joys of the senses, joy in general, things that God considers a vice.. and my nonconformist morality is not a means of obtaining something, it is an end."

"Did the fires of Hell not make you change your mind?"

Lucifer hesitated and spoke, with a voice that sounded like a sigh: "Perhaps the fires offered me that warmth that I was unable to find in heaven".

Audacious, careless and reckless, Sophia stayed inside the prison until late and Lucifer played with her like a cat plays with a mouse. Obscure words, paradoxes and strange insinuations that she didn't fully understand.

Before she left, he added: "I have other things to tell you, young woman, and I would be happy if you could return tomorrow. They haven't even allowed the moon to keep me company".

"I don't think I will be able to return," she said, but something stirred in her heart.

"I'm an exile in a foreign land, my chamber is among the stars and your eyes help me not to feel homesick."

A wrinkle appeared on her white forehead as something resurfaced from the oblivion of her memory, a distant memory, and the glimmer of a forgotten life emerged, but it was only for a moment.

"I will wait," he insisted.

Sophia left, saying nothing. The prisoner's words floated around her mind for a long time, silent words that brought a storm with them.

As he looked into her eyes, Lucifer saw the certainty that she would return.

∽ ∽ ∽

The following day, while the Sunday church bells were ringing with the same energy as an early morning rooster, Sophie stayed inside her hotel room, working hard on her interview with the Devil. Later on, she gave the piece to the editor-in-chief, who was astonished by it: "I didn't think you would really do it, young lady," he said. Arrangements were immediately made for a televised report to be put together.

During the recording made in prison, the Devil was not visible and appeared as a shadow beyond the glass, but his voice ringing out was unmistakable.

Her colleague Jim wanted to warn her: "Why did you risk so much, Sophia? Going down to his cell, speaking to him..."

"I don't think he's searching for souls right now," she replied.

"But you're playing with fire! The immortal soul is all we mortals possess."

"Yet a voice that has never been heard exists and has travelled through time, carried by the desert wind. I'm just doing my job, Jim. I'm honouring the Devil's word."

"But this is not a fairy-tale and the Devil is not a frog who will become a prince when kissed."

"Lucifer is already a prince!" she snapped, and then sighed. "Sorry, you're right. I don't know what's happening to me. He said a few things to me... as if he had always known me".

Jim grabbed her by the shoulders. "I worry about you, Sophia. Don't go back to that prison! Take a holiday, a long way from here, a long way from *him*".

"It's impossible to escape from doubt; it's inside me and it may always have been there. But you're right," she admitted, "I should get away."

That same evening, under a full moon that seemed to be brimming over, a cloud of bats fluttered noisily around the maximum security prison.

Annoyed, the director of the institute answered his phone, "What's going on?"

"Someone wishes to see the prisoner in cell 666, Sir" a policeman said, and the monitor in his office showed the image of Sophia Madlane, who was waiting to go in.

The director did not seem too surprised. "It's alright," he confirmed after some hesitation, "she came in yesterday too, she's got a permit. Let her in."

"But director…"

"No discussions. Check the courtyard. The dogs are restless this evening." He hung up the phone, with a slight moan, and beads of sweat were glistening on his forehead.

A large spider slowly walked across his shoulder and jumped onto the table. The director tried in vain to wriggle his way out of the spider's web in which part of his body was entangled.

"Excellent performance" Bensoria complimented herself, appearing out of the shadows. "The important thing now is that nobody goes to disturb the resident of cell 666."

"Free me, I beg of you…"

The witch got closer to him and her long red hair waved around like tentacles, caressing the back of the man's neck: "There's a night that needs to pass... "

The crow cawed outside the window.

∽ ∽ ∽

Several meters further down, Sophie had been let in by the guards and she walked down Lucifer's corridor. This time the accused's cell was completely dark and there was no music; the only sound coming from its occupant was his slow breathing in the centre of the room. When Sophia caught a glimpse of his outline, she realized that once again he was expecting her.

"I don't know why I've come back," she said, feeling somewhat uneasy.

The prisoner's voice replied from out of the darkness, "You knew that I've got more to tell you".

"But why to me in particular?" She twisted a rebellious lock of hair on her forehead. "I shouldn't even be here... my permit was for one day. I don't know why they let me in."

In the middle of the room, the Devil's eyes lit up. "Why don't you come in?" he asked her.

"What?"

"What are you afraid of? The serpent never attacks people except in self-defence." He had a bewitching smile on his face. "I am your unfulfilled dream, Sophia, the echo of silence, the thing you have always sought beneath the sky and above the moon, which you will never be able to find, because it does not exist."

Words like mazes confused her thoughts.

Sophia covered her face sensing strange memories reawakening inside her and an alien desire in her consciousness. Straining to fight it, she reacted by fleeing towards the end of the corridor where the guard had stopped to wait for her.

"Already back?" he asked.

Without thinking, Sophia punched him in the stomach and the guard collapsed, groaning. Then she hit him on the back of his neck and stunned him. Her heart was beating madly as she identified the right key on the guard's belt and inserted it into the computer control panel. Her gestures and movements were quick and out of her conscious control. Although she had never seen that contraption before, she was able to use it with remarkable skill, quickly deactivating the laser barrier and the security systems.

A few moments later, the door of cell 666 opened up with a swishing noise. The door of Hell, a door filled with darkness, was before her, inviting her to enter; the Pillars of Hercules of the conscience.

The woman hesitated, before letting herself be swallowed up.

Many floors higher up in the building, in the director's room, Bensoria had opportunely turned off the monitor linked to cell 666.

"It isn't appropriate to be too indiscreet, is it?" she said mischievously to the man.

"That woman is lost!"

In the cell, a whirlwind had welcomed the journalist, making her hair wave about, and she felt as if she had entered another dimension. She felt as if she were floating in the air, the damp air, and the floor felt soft, like a rippling firmament at her feet. Satan appeared at her side, as a slight glow made him recognizable; he took off her coat and put it on the edge of the bed, a nest of soot. She didn't try to resist, feeling lost in an environment that was much larger that its size when seen from the outside and in which it was impossible to see the boundaries; steamy fumes shone in the distance, while fireflies and will-o'-the-wisps hovered in the air.

"Have you ever danced on the edge of the abyss" he asked her, taking her hand and leading her to the middle of the cell, where music accompanied their steps.

Sophia half-closed her eyes and shivered as she felt her blouse slip away, exposing her bare skin. Her trousers seemed to have a will of their own as they fell from her legs onto the floor and her light camisole dropped, floating in the soft transparent light.

In the dimly lit room, the invisible light of the moon was reflected on Sophia's skin. For a moment, Satan stood still, observing the woman beside him, the shape of her body, her throbbing chest, her warm breath. Not even the Devil could stop time, as the sand in the hourglass slipped relentlessly between his fingers... but perhaps he could slow it down.

As a warm wind caressed the outskirts of the city, the demon's fingers caressed Sophia's hips; as lightning tore through the sky, his hands ran along her long legs; and as a light rain dampened the buildings, Satan's forked tongue touched her neck.

"It's in moments like these that I miss having a heart," he whispered.

Shaken by a quiver, the woman groaned, suddenly realizing what was happening: the depths closed in upon her; the heat of the flames was around her, making her feel dizzy.

She jumped in shock and began to retreat. "No!"

Leaning on the wall, with her chest dancing to the rhythm of her laboured breathing, she stared at the guest, who was looking at her innocently, with the innocence of someone who doesn't know the meaning of innocence.

Then she walked over to him, hesitant, lightly touched his face and hair and kissed him.

∽ ∽ ∽

Nobody passing by at that late hour would have noticed the layer of ice on the Limmat river trembling, cracking and then breaking below the Munsterbrucke bridge, as a diabolic figure emerged from the waters and stood drying its wings in front of the city buildings. The moon was obscured by a blanket of clouds blown by the breeze that night and a series of flashes of lighting announced a clap of thunder that awoke the night from its slumber. Hit by a bolt of lightning, the great clock on Saint Peter's bell tower exploded in a Catherine wheel of sparks. From the other side of the river, Asmodeus, the demon of art, taking no notice of the suddenly hostile weather, climbed up between the two twin spires of Grossmunster Cathedral to get his saxophone ready. His shadow moved along the Romanesque-Gothic pediment of the building, swaying in the wind and lit up by the lightning, while the sound of sweet, melancholic Blues, the music of the Devil, began to fill the air. Thousands of years before, Asmodeus had followed Lucifer in his rebellion, driven by his love of art: to be creative, it was necessary to reject one's state of being a creature.

Dogs howled in the streets, rats raced frantically through the sewers, something unmentionable was taking place and was transmitting a strange excitement everywhere. Abandoning himself to sensual pleasures that had remained dormant for so long, Lucifer's cold body met Sophia's warmth and, as in a dreamlike vision, the whole of cell 666 seemed to shake. The prisoner's bed rose up and began to float around the room, rotating and letting off an unreal glow. The wind panted, the sand dunes in the desert shook, the waves of the sea broke on the rocks, the Earth began to move more slowly. The encounter between Eve and the serpent had repeated itself.

When Asmodeus stopped playing, he bowed theatrically before an invisible audience in the city.

Lucifer's bed gently returned to the floor, allowing the two lovers to rest; Sophia was still, but the sea in her eyes was stormy with thoughts.

"The wolf shall dwell with the lamb, and the leopard shall lie down with the young goat," she said, remembering *Isaiah's* prophecy.

But Lucifer was far away, with his eyes closed, and he too was lost in ancient recollections.

"1572, 23 August… one night with no moon or stars."

"What?"

"There were rumours about you. They said you practiced magic and that you were the Devil's concubine."

"Me?"

"That you were a *witch*."

Staring at the Devil, for a fleeting moment Sophia remembered.

Like a flash of lightning shedding light on her memories, she saw herself with him.

"You're in my past…," she murmured in disbelief. "Oh, but how could that have happened?"

"The slaughter began in Paris, as the bells rang out. Crosses had been drawn on the houses to identify the infidels. King Charles IX's men went out into the streets armed with torches and swords, intent on exterminating the Huguenots and every enemy of the faith. The Holy Spirit sang within them. A massacre took place that night, the night before the feast of St Bartholomew, and a corner of the world became worse than my Hell."

"What are you talking about?"

The demon opened his eyes and his expression was one of endless melancholy.

"A group of religious worshippers burst into your house, surprising you as you performed an esoteric ritual and they took you to Place Maubert, where the fires were already burning."

"What are you saying?"

"You perished on the stake, Satia, along with other souls. Your cries reached the depths of the Underworld and echoed in my chest."

She turned pale: "I'm Sophia…"

"You were my witch, Satia. After your death I was unable to seduce any other women and, not long after that, witches became extinct... The inquisition was burning them all."

Sophia remembered more clearly. In sixteenth-century France, she had been Satan's lover and was condemned to be burned at the stake as a witch. Images flooded her mind: scenes of passion, pain and death.

She put her hands over her face: "Oh, but how is it possible?"

"A God who justified them, a God who absolved them, accomplice and instigator of their actions." He gently touched her white forehead, moving a lock of her coppery hair out of the way. "I've been awaiting your reincarnation for centuries, Satia. I waited for the tide of time to bring you back to me."

As she caressed his face, she caught a glimpse of the features of the angel he had once been.

"I too have been searching for you forever," she said in words mixed with sighs, "I have been chasing the shadow of a truth that never showed itself. Perhaps fate has something to do with this trial. It has allowed us to find each other again."

Lucifer raised his closed hand and his fist, suddenly white-hot, burst into flames. When the flames went out, a red rose appeared in the palm of his hand.

"A sort of magic spell," he said, with the hint of a smile.

She took the flower. It was a rose that seemed to throb like a human heart and a little stream of blood trickled from its petals.

"I lost my heart long ago," the prince whispered, "the only thing inside my chest now is the echo of immense, silent solitude."

Sophia placed her hand on his chest, where only silence could be heard. "So much suffering… let me give you my heart."

He took her hand, with his clawed fingers touching her white skin.

"You have already given it to me," he murmured.

18

The Devil's Word

Book of Jubilees 1:20, apocrypha

The eye of God rose majestically opening the doors of the dawn and lighting up that corner of the world with icy reality. While he put the parts of his saxophone back into its case, Asmodeus saw the light colouring the buildings and streets as they livened up. Sophia was going back into the city just as the newspapers were coming out, with the following headlines:

INTERVIEW WITH THE DEVIL, SATAN CONFESSES,
WORD OF THE DEVIL.

The evening before, the TV report on the interview prepared by her newspaper had been aired and was very successful. The Devil's voice had been added over file footage: crowded towns and deserts, wealth and poverty in the world, as a setting for his word, enriched by sequences taken from the trial and reprocessed on the computer. The *New York Times* had achieved a real triumph, beating all competition and putting Sophia on the pedestal of international journalism.

With copies of the newspapers in his hand and looking tense, Nick entered the studio, giving his associates a cursory greeting, and closed himself away in his room. He hadn't liked the TV report. He asked Linda to make him some tea and flipped through the articles; this wasn't what he had expected. His client hadn't respected the instructions.

On the other hand, Von Hugh seemed to appreciate it. "For thousands of years the sacred texts have been preserved in Latin to prevent people from understanding them and the truth was right there, under everyone's nose, but nobody was able to understand it. Now, the Devil's intervention has provided the right interpretation. God is naked before creation".

"But nobody can see him," detective Frank Moroni sniggered.

Some of the sentences in the interview caught the professor's eye. "Subversive thought, a lawless revolutionary who knows how to look into the depths of Hell without getting dizzy." He looked up: "Love for the world! This was the Devil's original sin: a love for creation more that for his creator".

Something suddenly stirred in the lawyer's mind. "But what if it's all a fraud? What if he's taking advantage of the stage so that he can preach? He could be using us to do something he wasn't able to do before: transvalue values, break the ancient tables, spread worldwide discord."

Victor stroked his beard, perplexed, and the others reflected: was the trial a clever trap set by the Devil to trick the world? How could man have captured evil without the help of supernatural forces? Who was the obscure director of the event, Heaven or Hell?

The Devil's irreverent laugh returned to their minds.

"So it's all a *bluff*, Mr Valance," Frank ventured, "from his capture, to judgement... all planned for his propaganda, so that he can gather proselytes."

Nick didn't like the idea of being a pawn in the game, but before he could reach a conclusion, a thundering voice outside caught his attention: "Valance, where are you? Is nobody here in this damned office?"

Linda went to open the door to a furious Bernard Louis who burst into the room, holding a copy of the *Neue Zurcher Zeitung*, Zurich's most longstanding newspaper. "Was it you who authorized this farce of an interview?" he snapped. "Was the live trial not enough for you?"

The assistants left them alone.

"The television distorts the content of the debate," Valance explained "and I thought an interview might be useful, but I'm disappointed with the result, too."

Louis grumbled, "Come on Valance, that's enough now. Did you think about a plea bargain?"

"A plea bargain?"

"Negotiating the Devil's penalty would already be a good victory for you. We can come to an agreement on the penalty and, later on, you could obtain house arrest in Hell for your client. What do you say? You will obtain the rehabilitation of your criminal."

Nick thought about the unexpected proposal, while Bernard stood before him with his hands on his hips. Then he decided. "Making a deal would disavow what has been said so far… and I doubt that my client would accept an agreement".

"But the acquittal of the Devil is a legal *monstrum*! Do you realize that if you were to win, the legality of the system would be turned upside-down? The legal system would never be the same again."

"That's not my problem."

"Careful, Valance," said the lawyer, pointing a finger at him, "if the law collapses, nobody will be safe anymore. Evil will be legitimized and you will be swept away by the same system that you are breaking up." He threw the newspaper in the air and walked off, muttering.

His words continued to spin around the lawyer's mind for a long time, with the lucid awareness that the magistrate was right.

∞∞∞

Madlane's interview was broadcast and repeated all over the world, causing inevitable controversies. From the top of the Eiffel tower, the preacher, Joe Pelton, announced once again and more vigorously this time: "The truth is clear for all to see: in reality, God is disguised as the Devil and he is subjecting the world to hardest of tests. Once upon a time he turned himself into a man, to save humanity, and now he has turned himself into the Devil to save the demons. All that remains for us to do is crucify him!"

In the Vatican, Teomondo III put down the report drafted by the Congregation for the Doctrine of the Faith, before scrutinizing the faces of the thirty cardinals sitting before him.

"Is this the result of your *inquirendum*?" he asked.

The cardinals nodded.

"What should I say *ex cathedra*, that the accused is the Antichrist? That he is the personification of Evil who has risen from the ashes?" he said impatiently: "What's being disputed here is not our enemy's identity, but the concept of the word *evil*." He banged his fist on the table. "Its concrete definition! The idea of sin is being doubted. The DNA of religions and the elementary code of the *word* are being attacked. Your report does not resolve the ethical problems that have been raised".

The prefect of the Congregation timidly cleared his throat, "Your Holiness, the Devil's declarations were too quick to allow us to come up with a timely reply.

Furthermore, the Church was not prepared to face the Devil in this way, a devil so... so..."

"So *human*?" Teomondo suggested, with a hint of sarcasm.

"Our worshippers are confused, and many are identifying with his words."

"Even Christ was a man," the Pope reminded him.

The prefect insisted: "Holiness, there is great rebellion within the clergy: the dioceses are having a crisis, the worshippers are criticizing us and abandoning us... and it isn't only about them. We are also losing priests, nuns and even bishops. We are exposed to the merciless judgment of the media." He looked at the Pope, with a hopeful expression in his eyes. "We think that the problem is common to all the great denominations and should be dealt with. I therefore renew my invitation to you to take the way of the ecumenicalism".

As the Pope knew, the last few weeks had been a disaster for every religion and not only because donations had decreased, but also because the religious leaders had lost control of the doctrine. Teomondo hid his face behind his bejewelled fingers. He had always rejected ecumenicalism, fearing that it might weaken his leadership and he now saw himself forced to take this road without any certainty regarding the outcome.

However, the prophecy of Fátima rang out relentlessly in its mind: "The ancient serpent is very slippery... slippery..."

He raised his head tiredly. "However, we will organize the work".

တ တ တ

An unrelenting drizzle dripped down the windows, marking the passing of time that seemed never-ending. When the telephone rang in Valance's office, a female voice on the other end of the line whispered languidly, "What do you think about a short truce, Mr Valance?"

Valance gave a little smile, recognizing her. "I'm sorry I was a little harsh during the last hearings. Would you like to go out for a drink and a chat Miss Brinne?"

"I thought we were on a first name basis?"

Later, Nick Valance and Natalie Brinne were seated in one of Zurich's typical local bars on the right bank of the Limmat river, sipping a drink and talking about their lives. Despite the light sleet, they had walked around for a while in the Hirschgasse, a narrow winding lane that climbed from the Limmat river to the Niederdorf, the most important pedestrian road in the old town, and they were on their way to the cafes and restaurants at the end of the street. With a friendly, accommodating tone of voice, Natalie was hoping to glean some information; Nick was hoping to do the same thing.

In the lounge of the bar, the soft lighting blurred the edges of the room and the slow music made it easy to shake off any tension.

"In this period, we all need a little relaxation," Natalie said, running a hand through her damp hair, causing a few snowflakes to fall from it. "Tell me about yourself, Nick. Are you married?"

"Yes, but my wife stayed in London. She doesn't like trials, and I don't like distractions. What about you? Are you married?"

"The last time I tried to live with a man, it only took me a week to scare him away!"

"You don't seem all that bad."

"I place a lot of importance on my job and neglect the rest."

Nick gave an understanding nod. "Are you of French origin?"

"Belgian, but I've been living here for years."

"What's it like working with your colleague, Louis?"

The woman smiled: "He may not seem it, but Bernard is very kind. He has taken this trial to heart. He's an idealist."

"A characteristic typical of inquisitors."

"Tell me something, Nick. It seems like there's something personal going on between you and God."

"Oh no," he said, denying it with a gesture, "I don't doubt his role of creator, but just that of legislator. God lets the crimes of the fathers fall onto the shoulders of their children "down to the third and fourth generation", something inconceivable for the law, because responsibility is personal. Then, he orders us not to kill, but he himself eliminates his opponents and forgives criminals just because they repent. If an authority is incapable of being coherent with its own principles, what principles can it impart?"

"I had never considered this point of view."

"Everything is founded on his discretionary power and not on the objectiveness of the law and, in this way, men become accustomed to asking for favours without ever becoming aware of their own rights."

Natalie put down her glass. "You are too rational, Nick".

"Oh, I'm just a lawyer," he replied.

"Anyhow, you have shown that you're skilful. Ironically, when faced with the Devil, we found ourselves in difficulty." The girl blinked: "Which is more important, good or God's omnipotence? If God were evil, should we give up on heaven to follow good or give up on good to follow God? These are very difficult problems".

"It's just a trial."

"However interesting it may be, I fear that your theory can never be demonstrated," the girl said, swallowing the last drop of her drink. "And we will be able to surprise you!"

Nick stared at the red of the wine, a small ocean of blood rippling in concentric circles. He wasn't accustomed to drinking alcohol, but that night he allowed his thoughts to come out. When the two of them left the bar, it was late. Natalie had hoped to get Nick drunk, but as they returned home, he was still lucid and she was tipsy. The lawyer had to accompany her to her flat and, out of professional ethics, he avoided snooping through her documents.

∽ ∽ ∽

The Devil fidgeted, annoyed, under the spotlights that morning. The bones in his face were showing through from beneath his taut muscles and sunken cheeks, while Bernard Louis subjected him to an intense interrogation. The interview with the Devil had raised problems of how to formulate the charges and made a specific confrontation on the topic of morality necessary.

When Natalie Brinne entered the courtroom to take her place, she glanced casually at Nick Valance, who was sitting at his bench, looking unruffled.

"Do you deny that the heavenly Father loves us?" Bernard asked, walking up and down in front of the accused. "Do you deny the miracles performed for us?"

"Objection" Valance intervened. "Miracles are alterations of the rules of the world to the advantage of single individuals, who often declare themselves to be unworthy, and they represent a disparity with regard to the treatment of others."

The observation did not cause the public prosecutor to lose his composure and, motionless before the accused, he continued to stroke his large jaw. "You have no feelings, do you?"

Not having agreed upon anything with his client, Nick felt tense: the subject of feelings was extremely popular.

But the Devil was indifferent. "Feelings cloud your judgment. If God loved you, he could not judge you".

Thoughts rippled like waves through the audience and the temperature in the room dropped abruptly.

Trying to touch a raw nerve, Bernard said, "Yet, God respects human freedom, which you continuously violate with your temptations".

"Freedom?" The Devil scratched the arms of his chair: "You want to teach me about freedom? I gave up heaven for freedom and no hell has induced me to repent! I am fighting against the greatest limit to human freedom: divine omnipotence".

"But the morality you teach is against nature!"

"What do you mean by against nature?" the Devil said rebelliously, and his breath was the only breath that produced no steam. "Perhaps progress and civilization are based on nature? All of human history is against nature. I am trying to free to you from the merciless nature in which God has imprisoned you!"

The judge invited the accused to express himself in a more understandable way, and Valance was annoyed. He had always advised his client not to make personal attacks. "Never attack God or your accusers," he had urged, "leave that job to me."

Lucifer noticed that the lawyer was staring at him with an air of reproach and he stopped talking. Around them, the cold had become biting: the frost was making lacy patterns of ice on the window panes.

The judge deemed it necessary to suspend the hearing and the sound of his gavel dissolved the atmosphere.

Slightly embarrassed, Natalie approached the defence's bench. "I'd like to say sorry for yesterday, Nick," she said. "I don't know what got into me... I usually don't drink alcohol."

"I exaggerated too," he confessed. "It was a pleasant exaggeration though."

She smiled, but there was no space for any other comments, because the plaintiff's lawyer, Gonzales, spoke, announcing an imminent initiative.

"Ladies and gentlemen, I have been given the task of informing you that the various religions have accepted Pope Teomondo's proposal and the first interdenominational conference of all the religions has been called: an opportunity to reverse the scenario."

19

God's design

> Seek not to be judge, being not able to take away iniquity.

Sirach 7:6

Before a red, setting sun, the Swissair aircraft moved smoothly along the runway of the Zurich Kloten airport, coming from the East. From the ladder of the aircraft, the Dalai Lama, smiling in his saffron-coloured robes, looked out to greet the crowd below. He had initially refused to participate in a frivolous event like a trial, but ethical needs required his presence: the recent hearings had produced a deep split within the religious communities and the world seemed incapable of reacting. As usual, it was left up to the men of faith to rectify human failures.

The invitation to the interdenominational congress of the faiths had reached him from the Pope in person, who had suggested "burying thousands of years of incomprehension in favour of superior moral unity". He had felt that it was his duty to offer the Western World this opportunity.

That same evening, the religious leaders met in the Kongresshaus, the Congress Palace on the lakefront, to try to develop a common ethic with which they could oppose the Devil's position. In over three thousand years of faith, an agreement had never been reached and the plaintiff's attorney, Gonzales, who was acting as a coordinator, didn't hold out much hope. But the crisis was now conditioning all aspects of global society, making participation necessary.

With father Cimor by his side, Teomondo III browsed through the speech prepared for him by his staff. The Holy Spirit seemed to be hovering around him under the form of incense fumes. He closed the report without reading it and looked at the attendees for a long time.

The Archbishop of Canterbury was also present and had accepted the invitation to clarify her position. Known for her forward-thinking ideas, Lady Marian was the only woman present and this created a certain distrust. Ever since Henry VIII had founded the Anglican religion in the sixteenth century, the English Church had kept its distance from other Protestant denominations and had developed autonomously. Lady Marian had become archbishop only a few months before, as the result of the controversial reform that had opened up the doors of priesthood to women.

"The fallen angel is trying to get up again, ladies and gentlemen," said the Vicar of Christ. "The ancient antagonist of religions, the enemy of every divine mystery, is near us and is challenging us to demonstrate our strength. If the word of God created the world, the word of the Devil wants to destroy it. We cannot remain indifferent to this challenge. We need to establish a dialogue, cooperation between the different faiths with the aim of defeating the common enemy. I have always been a fervent supporter of ecumenicalism, and not *ab intra* ecumenicalism concentrating on Christianity, but ecumenicalism *ab extra* aimed at all the religious communities in the world. Only this ethic will allow us to defeat Satan and make him return to his eternal prison."

Those present gave their unanimous approval.

"Several prophecies had already announced judgment on the angels and the imprisonment of the Devil. But another one exists." With a troubled air, the Pope pulled out a yellowed letter and delicately lay it on the bookstand. It was the first time that anything like this had taken place. "I will trust in your secrecy." Frowning, with hesitant fingers, he cleared his throat and began to read. "In recent days, the devil's last days, the creature of evil, Satan, will come to Earth overflowing with anger and will be captured by man..."

The others began to squirm nervously, unable to understand what it was about.

"Human justice will have the opportunity to judge him and punish him for his foul crimes."

Some of the people present turned pale.

"... but the ancient serpent is very astute and very slippery... "

"What is it about," rabbi Tariz asked, "and what does it mean?"

"What prophecy is this?" the Muslim imam asked, echoing the rabbi's words.

"Fátima…," father Cimor exclaimed, sensing the truth. "Is it the prophecy of Fátima, Holiness?"

Teomondo folded the letter up and carefully put it away: "The third prophecy of Fátima, ladies and gentlemen, which had never before been disclosed, has, as you can see, come true".

He had finally done it. He had revealed the terrible secret. He had shared the weight of the cross he was bearing with the others.

There was a sudden commotion, with many of those present feeling afraid and a few even left; a mysterious divine plan had been revealed to them.

"Had the Vatican possessed this prophecy regarding the trial and kept it hidden until now?" the orthodox patriarch asked, indignant. "This is scandalous!"

"The Roman curia owes us an explanation!" the protestant pastor threatened.

"The Holy See was not authorized to disclose it," Teomondo said in his defence, "the prophecy belongs to God."

God's other representatives felt injured, humiliated and confused. Then the Archbishop of Canterbury, in her purple gown, asked to speak. "Dear Pontiff, the Virgin's prophecy is of no help to us. The situation is also serious because of the behaviour of the religious leaders. The Devil has undoubtedly lied and slandered God, who, being love itself, can only have mankind's freedom and happiness at heart. Thousands of years have passed since his personification and the law of God, like everything else, is subject to change. We cannot continue to look back at the past: a Third kingdom is needed, a Brand New Testament that is in step with the times".

The Dalai Lama approved with a smile: "If a new ethic needs to be written, we can provide a contribution".

The pastor of the Protestant Church, keeping an open mind, also agreed: "The latest truth is always the best. It's only right to look for it".

"But Allah's law cannot be changed" the imam said sternly, "it is an absolute law and if He does not change it, it means it's right for him the way it is."

"Perhaps God wants to leave this task up to us," Lady Marian suggested, "and wants to put our maturity to the test."

"Perfect!" the plaintiff's attorney Gonzales said, jumping at the idea. "With this approach, we could overturn the accusations. If we admit that God's morality is how Lady

Marian describes, the Devil will be proven wrong and will have to answer to slander!"

Teomondo did not hide his annoyance. "Admitting a morality different from that passed down is the same as yielding to the Devil and to secularization. A judicial victory would not compensate for the moral defeat".

However, his firmness triggered further dissent and the Protestant pastor grabbed hold of the cross: "During the period of the Great Reform, Luther accused the Pope of being the Antichrist!"

"Martin Luther was excommunicated," the Pope pointed out.

Using all of his diplomatic skills, the lawyer, Gonzales, was able to mitigate the different positions and, after extenuating discussions, the interdenominational congress was able to make a rough draft of a memorandum of understanding: a sort of ecumenical transaction between all the various religions. The basic agreement was found in the submission to divine will, whatever that was. Other points were identified in the affirmation that all religions are equal before God and that human evolution is guided by Providence. With such a flexible approach, the lawyer believed that a victory was possible, but all the religions would have had to give up their claim to universality.

That same night, intercontinental telephone calls and feverish negotiations filled the heavens, weaving together the undecipherable threads of Providence. The opportunity to bring the sacred laws together in a single design excited some but worried others. With *syncretism*, God's face would become a mosaic of different colours and images, the final physiognomy of which was difficult to predict.

The next morning, as an unusual sun lit up the Swiss metropolis, a satisfied lawyer, Gonzales, went to the courthouse to deposit the settlement. The streets were not busy and the thousand thoughts running through the man's mind made him distracted but aware of the fact that he was holding a document that could subvert the trial. He didn't notice the black BMW that was following him at a distance.

As he was about to cross the Hirschengraben, the car accelerated rapidly. Gonzales only noticed it when it was a few metres away from him: it was like a huge snorting, menacing bull. His mind went back to his youth, when he had been a *matador* in the Spanish arenas, and a word appeared on his lips: "*Olé…*" He was knocked down noisily in front of the entrance of the palace of justice and his body was thrown onto the pavement.

The car sped away in the distance as the screams of passers-by were lost in the Rämistrasse traffic.

∽ ∽ ∽

The news of the attack on the plaintiff's lawyer shook the public, as nobody could have imagined such consequences and, above all, the public prosecutor's office, which had pinned their hopes on him for a unified line of attack. The agreements between the religions collapsed and the opportunity to create a universal ethic was lost. The "ecumenical fundamentalists", an across-the-board inter-religious movement claiming to have carried out the attack, had won.

Closing an old book of medieval encyclicals, Sophia Madlane tidied up the reference books piled on the table. The night had spread its dark cape over the Predigerkirche building, where the central library of Zurich was located and where the journalist was intent on consulting ancient documents to find information supporting her theories. Frowning, her lips repeated silent thoughts, as the yellowed pages passed before her eyes. It was dangerous ground and she knew it, but she wanted to continue: she wanted to dig deep into dust-covered eternities and remember the moments she had experienced with Lucifer centuries before.

"If you want to find the source, you need to swim against the current," *he* had told her.

She pulled out her mobile phone and dialled her colleague's number.

"I'm in the library, Jim... listen to this: I've found some interesting material..." She held the telephone between her shoulder and her ear. "In the Bible, God orders the stoning of the rebel spirits and unleashed his rage against his people every time they turn to worship another divinity. The famous commandment "thou shalt have no other gods before Me" is evidence of his hostility towards every form of freedom. The same revelation can be seen as an attack against human freedom."

"What are you trying to prove, Sophia?" her colleague asked.

"In the *Syllabus of Errors*, Pope Pius IX condemned the principles of liberalism and modernity, including the concept of democracy." She continued to flip through other documents: "In the New Testament, the term "servant" is used more than one hundred and twenty times and the origin of the word *Muslim* is "submission". That same submission recommended in *St Peter's First letter*. "Be submissive to every human institution for the love of the Lord; domestic servants, submit yourselves to your masters with all respect"."

"You are getting too involved, Sophia... you should forget about this story."

She put down the books. "*Omnis potestas a Deo*, "the only authority is God". Do you understand what this means? The purpose of everything is social control"".

Her colleague remained silent for a few moments. "Sophia, don't jump to hasty conclusions."

"Is it God who uses the Churches to build his kingdom or the Churches that use God to build theirs? The end and the means are inextricably intertwined."

No answer came to that conjecture, and there was suddenly silence over the telephone. "Jim, are you still there?" The connection seemed to have been interrupted. Sophia tried to dial the number again, but she was distracted by a sudden noise. Looking around, she noticed that she was alone in the large room. It was later than she thought. Sitting at a table at the back of the room, there was a strange individual dressed in dark clothes with a cigar between his lips that were hidden by a black beard, with half of his face hidden by the shadows.

When the woman put down the textbooks, having decided to leave, the stranger watched her walking away and also got up. The strange individual went over to the table where she had been sitting, picked up a book that had fallen and, with clawed fingers, put it back on the shelf.

Worried about the absence of any caretakers, Sophia walked along the deserted corridors of the library. When she realized she had gone down the wrong corridor, she walked back and took another. With the dim lighting in that place, bizarre shadows seemed to decorate the walls and the woman thought she could hear someone saying her name: slow, deep whispers, but she couldn't work out where they were coming from.

"Learn to read between the unwritten lines in the ancient texts."

She shuddered at the thought of a man's footsteps behind her. Her heart was pounding and she ran along the endless labyrinths of criminal records in a building that seemed transformed, like moving tentacles. Several minutes went by before she could find the entrance hall, where the caretaker was mumbling in his sleep at the desk.

She went outside into the square, where a pale moon crossed the tattered shreds of a cloud, laying out a silvery blanket. She breathed a sigh of relief, before crossing over to the other side of the road.

Behind her, on the doorstep of the building, the stranger observed her as he lit a cigar with a click of his fingers. That girl needed protection, he thought, and it was up to him to be her guardian devil.

Adjusting the cloak on his shoulders, the demon Astaroth set off behind her.

ഗ ഗ ഗ

In the cathedral of Notre Dame in Paris, the sound of rock music rang out loud and clear amidst the frescoes on the dome. Those who believed in the defendant's innocence, meaning the part of the public seduced by the Devil, had organized a big charity concert in the Temple of Reason, in honour of the accused, with a collection of signatures in favour of his release.

Surrounded by the ancient mosaics in the naves, the devil Asmodeus stood invisibly with the mythical figures that adorned them and admired the public having fun to the notes of *Sympathy for the Devil.* In the lyrics of the songs, there were messages that he hoped would influence the listeners' unconscious minds. The future of Hell, he thought, also relied upon those dances.

At the same time, in Lourdes, a solemn mass with a vigil in favour of God had been organized, since everyone felt the need for the intervention of a *deus ex machina* in order to get things back into shape. Officiated over by several church-leaders, by the Catholic Pope, the Orthodox Patriarch and the Evangelical Pastor of the Protestant Churches, the mass brought together the world's major Christian communities in a single event, the only ecumenical demonstration accepted by the respective leaders.

Multiple sacred initiatives took place during those hours. At the Mecca, the Muslims united in prayer in the *Kaaba* around the Black Stone, the sacred object donated to Abraham by the angel Gabriel. In Rome, a sea of pilgrims besieged Saint Peter's Square with chants and prayers. In Salt Lake City, capital of the Mormon State of Utah, a large number of people arrived to defend the country from the imminent attack by the Devil. Television channels all over the world broadcast the spectacles on different channels and, during those few hours, the world was spiritually united by fear and by the wait for the verdict.

The blue Mercedes moved slowly and silently along the half-deserted streets of Zurich that evening, following its target. On the glistening road, Nick Valance was returning on foot from the courthouse where he had worked until late. He had refused the escort made available to him by the United Nations, feeling the need to walk alone, and the evening curfew established a few weeks before had made the city extremely safe.

When the car drove alongside the pavement and two individuals got out, the lawyer realized that he had been careless.

"Someone would like to speak to you, Mr Valance."

"Who are you?"

Without beating around the bush, the two individuals invited him to get into the car, in a way that allowed no objections.

The Mercedes set off again and, for about ten minutes, it sailed along the streets of the city centre in silence, until it stopped at the entrance to an imposing building on which there were numerous international flags.

Nick was taken inside, where a lift took him to the top floor. On the threshold, a short, bald man wearing wide glasses and who looked kind, was waiting for him.

"Welcome, *Herr* Valance" he said, with a friendly smile, "I'm glad you accepted my invitation."

"I was unable to say no," Nick said, suspiciously, "is this an abduction?"

"Oh, no" the little man assured him in a conciliatory tone of voice. "You are the Devil's defender. All the spotlights are on you. You are untouchable. We have only called you to talk. "

"Who are you?"

"My name is not important. I'm a coordinator. After you." The little man took Nick into a modern office. "What you see here is the control room. It controls part of the world. The world's balance also depends on these little lights."

Nick observed the electronic map of the world on the wall... an artificial firmament, a small paradise of omnipotence.

Then the little man took him to a large glass window, from which he could admire a view of the city, and offered him a drink.

"The Devil's testimony has considerably shaken the political ecosystem" he said, "and has endangered world security."

"I didn't imagine it would have effects like these."

"The Devil is spreading a dangerous culture." The dapper little man paused for a moment. "Human beings tend to be anarchical and state law alone is not enough to control them. A superior law is required... a law that promises stricter punishments than the human ones and big rewards for those who comply. A *divine* law." He gestured with one of his hands. "Religions also serve this purpose:

they regulate certain social balances and maintain a *status quo*".

"So, theology is an instrument for consolidating the authority of those who govern?" Nick said, warily.

The little man shrugged. "God is the king of kings, the monarch par excellence, and he doesn't legislate by consulting a database, because his power is born of itself. You will have noticed that in the Biblical Decalogue, men's duties are listed, but there is no mention of their rights…"

Nick stroked the back of his neck, as his thoughts meandered in the darkness.

"Keep the king's command, because of God's oath to him" says the book of *Ecclesiastes*, and according to the book of *Wisdom*, "Listen therefore, O kings, and understand; For your dominion was given you from the Lord and your sovereignty from the Most High". From up above in the heavens, God governs all of creation, eternal and unchanging."

Nick stared at the bottom of his glass. "But my client does not pursue any political ends."

"Your client wants to emancipate the men of God, but as well as being utopian, it is also wrong. The masses do not want to be free. They fear freedom and responsibility. They need to delegate their own salvation to someone. They need to be guided, because as well as not knowing where to go, they would not know how to do so either."

The little man's words fell coldly in the silence of the room.

Shaking his glass to make the ice cubes clink, Nick looked at the city lights. Something was stirring uneasily inside him.

"Unfortunately, state and culture are antithetical," the voice continued. "One lives and prospers at the expense of the other. In order to nourish the state, it is necessary to diminish the intellectual power of the people. Democracy is not compatible with religion, Mr Valance: it isn't possible for the will of the people and the will of God to exist at the same time, as each has interests that are irreconcilable with one another."

St Augustine's saying, "God is best known in not knowing him", made its way through the lawyer's mind.

"That's how the world is made, *Herr* Valance," the little man said, passing judgement, "from heaven to Earth, to the depths of the underworld; the same laws and the same rules. But you can render a useful service: speak to your client, explain this requirement to him, convince him to withdraw! Try to silence that demon."

Nick said nothing. The transparent, golden liqueur swayed around his glass.

"Why don't you help us? You too could have the opportunity to press some of those buttons in the control room..."

The lawyer looked at the lights on the nearby control panel. Betray his client, the symbol of immorality, with other immorality...

When he looked at his listener, the expression in his eyes was still professional: "I have always believed in values like respect for the law and for the rules. And for this reason, I'm sure you will understand that I cannot go back on a commitment I made".

He put down his drink, which he had not touched, and got up. He left giving the hint of a goodbye.

Through thick glasses, the little man watched him go through the door and disappear down the corridor. Then he turned to the lights of the buttons that were flashing on and off. Everything could be controlled from there, except for the individual.

He drank the last drop of his drink.

∽ ∽ ∽

When Frank Moroni entered the studio in the Weinplatz, it was the middle of the night. The lawyer's room was in semi-darkness, with just the table lamp on, and Nick was sprawled in an armchair in the corner of the room.

"Hello boss," Frank said, "sorry for following you... I saw you get back and I wanted to know if you needed anything."

Frank had been like Valance's guardian angel for years, appearing and disappearing at the most unusual times.

Nick shook his head feebly. There was an empty bottle of cognac cradled in his arm and his eyes were shining in the darkness. Frank realized that he was drunk.

"This case goes beyond my abilities," he murmured faintly. "When I accepted it, I didn't imagine that I would find myself involved in a war of these proportions."

"If there's something I can do...," Frank said, offering to help, even though he didn't have the faintest idea what Valance was talking about.

"They warned me: it's a plot, a trick... and I'm just a lawyer. Yet an immense world exists beyond the law... Do you know what I think?" he added, looking at the detective, "that, in the end, there is no proof that the rebel angel was defeated by God in the ancient rebellion. It's possible that he won...and now he could be there, sitting on the heavenly throne, without revealing his identity to anyone. While God, transformed into a demon, is forced to live on Earth, persecuted and hated by men, trying to communicate his truth. How would we know?" He looked at his friend with a tired expression: "I'm not God, Frank... nor the Devil,"

Frank replied, "There's a saying you repeat quite often, boss, when you're having problems... It was a saying of a certain... I can't remember... "

"Ferdinand of Habsburg," Nick suggested, smiling.

"Maybe, what was it now...?"

"Fiat iustitia et pereat mundus."

"And what does it mean?"

"May justice be done and let the world perish."

Frank tried to memorize it. Nick fell silent and looked serious as he stared into the emptiness, while the phrase echoed loud and clear in his head. The confident lawyer in him came to the fore again. A law existed and applying it was his job - the rest was not his responsibility.

He nodded a few times, then closed his eyes and the bottle slipped away. Frank looked at him, undecided about what to do. Hearing him breathing heavily, he got a cover and put it gently over his body. He turned off the light before leaving.

Somewhere outside, in the city, it sounded like a saxophone was playing.

∽ ∽ ∽

With a light swishing of wings, Asmodeus brushed up against Valance's building. With his saxophone in his arms, the demon circled and spun audaciously over the sleeping city, playing indefinable Blues music. His taut, slow, silent wings moved through the light air, keeping close to the buildings and gliding mysteriously around them. The notes rang out, distorted and confused by the wind, but were perfectly clear when they reached cell 666 at the maximum security prison, concealing a message that only the prince of demons could recognize.

Satan was perched on the ceiling of his cell, annoyed as he listened to the melody: He didn't like the message it was conveying.

Despite his opposition, the demons had continued to dig an underground tunnel under the prison and were determined to free him. Astaroth and Asmodeus had taken responsibility for this choice. They had always been rebellious devils.

Very soon the floor of the cell began to vibrate and crack: the last brick was taken away and the metal sheet perforated. Two holes formed in the ground and, with a dusty explosion, Barbatos's horns burst into the room.

"Prince, it's me," the demon bellowed, shaking his taurine head. "We've found you! This is the third attempt…" He rubbed his hoof on his face: "We allowed other prisoners to escape by mistake, but in the end we found you. Now, in a few minutes we are going to free you".

Lucifer sprang down from the ceiling. "I ordered you not to carry out your plan, Barbatos".

"But… the Great Council is worried and the whole of Hell demands that you return."

"As I said, I do not intend to escape."

The demon stared at his leader. "Why?"

"By escaping I will be losing more than my life... I will lose my pride, the real cause of my rebellion."

"But along with you, Hell will be lost too."

"You will continue your journey without me. Astaroth and Asmodeus will be valid heirs: they possess rationality and imagination, they do not need anything else. As far as I'm concerned, if I should die, I could become the symbol that I never was while I was alive."

"Martyrdom has always been against our immorality" the other demon said. "By remaining here, you are behaving like Socrates, or Jesus Christ."

"What?" Lucifer said, seizing the demon by the throat. "Don't you dare make comparisons!"

"Please forgive me..."

"Now go" the great rebel concluded, "the choice has been made. Lucifer will not go back."

Barbatos rubbed his aching neck and excused himself timidly, muttering as he disappeared. The demons in charge of digging the tunnel began to close the hole back up.

When the guards went to collect the accused around dawn, he was waiting for them in silence, standing in the middle of the room, with a detached expression. The music being broadcast via the cable radio was the sonorous *Also sprach Zarathustra* by Strauss.

Heading off towards his destiny, he murmured: "*Ecce diabolus*".

20

The verdict

The prince of this world now stands condemned.

Gospel according to John 16:11

A whirlwind of clouds rolled around an unnatural electric blue sky above the palace of justice, where a large deployment of anti-riot forces was separating the crowd of those who believed the Devil guilty from those who believed him innocent. Inside the building, there was a lot of tension, but also a lot of tiredness. The revelation had been personified and a merciless judgment had been passed on the world; thousands of years of spirituality had been soiled by the dark side of the heavens. A few hours before, a theological commission from Jerusalem had disseminated a bulletin urging for a conviction, fearing a possible early apocalypse.

When the light came on, the international connection was under way and Sophia Madlane, who had been given permission to comment on the last hearing, began. "Here we are at the last stage of the trial, the outcome of which is impossible to predict. Those in favour of the accused include the Satanists and also part of the scientific and intellectual world, while the governments and major religions are in favour of the prosecution. The millenarian sects appear to be divided: some maintain that the Devil is the

Antichrist who has come to undermine humanity, others that he is the messiah of a new alliance. We, the ordinary people, simple extras in this great tragicomedy, can do nothing but helplessly wait for history to take its course and for Justice and the Truth to be established by a human tribunal".

The view widened, showing the guest next to the woman. "We have the expert witness for the defence with us, professor Von Hugh, from whom we will push for something more on this story. What can be said at the end of this event? In reality, who or what is the Devil?"

The television cameras zoomed in on the philosopher while he stroked his beard. "We can see the Devil as a monster, an enemy to fight, or like a sick angel who needs love in order to shine again. But probably he is neither of the two." He blew smoke into the air. "The Devil is just someone whose opinion differs from God's. He is different, an antithesis. In this trial, today, for the first time an attempt has been made to legitimize the right to diversity."

When the judge entered the courtroom, all attention was again focused on the trial. Tom Salomon seemed tired but satisfied. It was the last hearing of the trial and perhaps of his life. The sitting was declared open and he immediately gave the floor to the prosecution for the closing speech.

Approaching the members of the jury, Bernard Louis's robust figure took up the entire image on the television screen. "I will say only a few words, ladies and gentlemen. During this trial, the accused has judged and condemned God. But he only did it to absolve himself. What is the reason for moral judgment on God, given that he is the only God in existence? Nobody can expect that the Absolute be made in his own image. God is "He who is", and we have a huge debt with him: the debt of existence."

He turned to the lawyer. "Man is not able to distinguish good from evil and has to trust in the word of God, in his judgement criteria and in his omniscience. And nobody is justified in judging divine law, since it is a super-constitutional law! "For us, justice will entail putting all these commands into practice, before God, as he ordered us to do", according to the Book of *Deuteronomy*, the most ancient source of law".

He pointed at the accused: "Since the time of Adam and Eve, the evil one has never changed his nature: he is and will remain evil, the enemy of God and of whomever believes in him. His words seduced humanity at the beginning of time and today he has tried to do the same thing. Therefore, do not listen to him. Listen to the voice of your conscience, the cries of your conscience demanding justice. Even those who have had no religious education know that the Devil is evil. No sophism, no dialectics and no philosophy can change that. The Devil was weakened by the reincarnations of Buddha, by the resurrection of Christ, by the birth of Mohammed and by the work of all the prophets. Now we can inflict the final blow upon him. Humanity is called upon for this task: this is the only way it can redeem itself from evil. Once its personification has been eliminated, evil will disappear from the world and we will all be able to return to the Garden of Eden from which we came, a heaven without apples and without serpents. Therefore, condemn the accused without any extenuating circumstances and remember that not only are we being watched on TV worldwide but we are undoubtedly also being watched from Heaven and a final verdict is being awaited. Let us demonstrate that we are his children".

The liberating applause that followed made the windows vibrate and tears of commotion spread throughout the audience.

When it was the defence's turn, Nick Valance got up and adjusted his gown. He had worked industriously for the last few days, to complete the closing argument and the critics were eager to listen to it. Everyone observed him nervously as he approached the jury.

"Ladies and gentlemen of the jury, in recent months, we have listened to a strange truth, a new truth, a truth that is uncomfortable for some, incredible for others and undoubtedly disturbing for everyone. When put on the scales, the sacred texts weigh more, but the Devil's word cannot be ignored. And the Devil's word has revealed today that which no prophet had ever done before: God's design. The design of that same divinity that, with eternity and omnipotence at his disposal, could have created a perfect world, if he had wanted to. Instead, he created a world that required prohibition and supervision and that degenerated at the first lack of attention: it was soon full of diseases, suffering, the law of the strongest, natural selection and death. The truth is that God did not want to create a perfect world, because he would have become useless in a perfect world. God created an imperfect world to give a meaning to his perfection."

There was murmuring in the audience and the judge wearily covered his face. The lawyer continued to speak with words that seemed inspired. "And Mr Yahweh, the God of the Jews, the Lord of the armies, did not generate perfect beings like himself to fill the universe, beings equal to him with whom he could share eternity. He made inferior beings out of mud, weak and dependent beings, he did not create the world to satisfy the desires of his creatures, but to satisfy his own. "I only created demons and men so that they would adore me" the Koran reveals; and "the Father is seeking such people to worship him" according to the Gospel. And therefore, if this is the kingdom of God and if this is the Promised Land, I disassociate myself from it, I rebel against him!"

He pointed a finger at the sky: "I accuse God of having taken advantage of man, conspiring against his happiness, of having given greater importance to his apples than to his children! I accuse him of having hindered human growth for fear of losing control of his kingdom and of having used the Devil as a scapegoat, like a fig leaf, to hide his own mistakes and injustices. I also accuse the religions of having been the tool of the divine design and his secular arm".

The audience's discord forced him to stop and the judge made a vain attempt to restore silence.

The lawyer's words were once more like sword thrusts as he continued, "If God were really good, there would be no need for intercessions or prayers in order to get his attention. The proof in favour of the accused is this: if there is more evil than good in the world, it is because Lucifer was defeated in his fight against Heaven; because God is stronger than the Devil!"

Everyone in the room was dumbfounded, offended, incredulous; a closing argument that went beyond all expectations. Several religious leaders stood up to protest and the guards intervened to restore order.

Valance waited for the silence to return, then carried on: "But there have been a few men, who were mistreated and misunderstood, who fought to improve this world... men inspired by the Devil, who searched for the tree of knowledge in order to find the lost paradise again and to whom our civilization is indebted. Now we must continue so that the sacrifice made by Adam and Eve was not in vain. They gave up the tree of life for the tree of knowledge: they gave up immortality for the freedom of future generations. If you are their children, demonstrate that you know the difference between good and evil".

A feeble applause followed, along with some approval, and the judge turned to the devil: "Does the accused have something to say before the final verdict?"

Satan half-closed his eyes: "God created mankind in his own image; but I civilized mankind".

After that, the members of the jury retired to deliberate.

"Excellent closing argument, boss," a moved Frank said, complimenting Valance.

"You seemed possessed, Mr Valance," his secretary Linda said, "as if you were inspired…"

Nick smiled, "That's exactly the impression I wanted to give".

ᔕ ᔕ ᔕ

The jury, which was made up of worshippers belonging to various religions, as well as a couple of atheists and agnostics, included twenty-one members from different parts of the world… twenty-one souls to whom the fate of justice was linked. They met and discussed the trial records: they spoke of the death penalty, rehabilitation and life imprisonment. There had been numerous attempts to put pressure on them in recent days. The last happening had occurred the previous night, when they had all had terrible nightmares.

While the journalists had been carrying out opinion polls on the outcome of the event, Nick and Bernard Louis met casually at the courthouse bar and had a drink together, exchanging very few words. They were no longer antagonists and were surprised to find that they had a great many things in common.

The verdict was destined to be reached quite quickly. The first timid signs of spring were appearing in the greyness of the city when a public announcement was made, following a gruelling closed session of deliberation, indicating that the verdict was imminent. The media's attention was reawakened. The London bookmakers and the clandestine betting market had seen huge fortunes being moved in recent days.

It was a Saturday morning and the live television coverage opened with focus on the members of the jury as they appeared in the courtroom, taking their places in the jury box. Tension was sky high everywhere. Even the Devil in his cell appeared to be as pale as a corpse.

Making everyone present stand, the judge asked, "Has the jury reached a verdict?"

"Yes," the president of the jury replied with an ill-concealed sigh.

An envelope was given to Tom Salomon, who opened it before the eager eyes of the television cameras. He pulled out the typewritten sheet of paper and, with slightly clouded vision, he read it out loud: "In the name of the sovereign people. Judicial proceeding number 666: The international community against Lucifer Satan, known as Beelzebub, prince of Hell. Charge: having damned the world". He cleared his throat: "The jury of the people: having examined the trial records, assessed the evidence from the trial, listened to the theories of the prosecution and of the defence, seen the articles of the criminal code, with votes cast by secret ballot resulting in 11 to 10, hereby delivers the following verdict: the jury recognizes the accused..."

The judge coughed and suddenly felt ill, forcing him to interrupt: with his hands on his chest, he began to gasp for air. A doctor was called, while the world's heart risked stopping along with that of the judge.

Then Salomon recovered, drank some water and swallowed a few pills. He took a deep breath and made sure he felt better. With trembling hands, he picked up the document and continued to read the ruling: "The jury... recognizes the accused... responsible for the temptations... but declares him not guilty of the charge of having damned the world, as this deed does not constitute a criminal offence".

Countless cries of surprise, some timid applause and endless whistling and booing in protest exploded in the room. The journalists exclaimed dumbfounded, "An acquittal! The most clamorous acquittal in history, a verdict that it will make future generations talk!"

Nick Valance smiled, while his assistants hugged each other before the flashes of the photographers' cameras: the Satanist Mirakis kissed Linda, Frank Moroni slapped Von Hugh on the back. At the prosecution bench, Bernard stood stunned by the news, clenching his huge jaw, and Natalie fell back onto her chair. In the audience, an astonished father Cimor stared at his silver crucifix, as if waiting for an explanation.

A moment later, as if in the grip of an earthquake, the building shook and the symbol of Justice, the golden scales, came off and fell crashing to the floor.

As the Blue Helmets intervened, trying to evacuate the building, the judge strained to read a few extracts of the motivation: "On the ancient rebellion of the angels against God, as it regards a matter reserved to divine law, the jury declares its lack of jurisdiction… The knowledge of good and evil, the premise and basis of law, cannot constitute a criminal offence... Although he tempted men, the Devil cannot be held responsible for the consequences, as man is capable of understanding and taking action and is the master of his own actions; the law assumes human responsibility and there are no exonerating or extenuating circumstances for those who are tempted by the evil one." The sheet of paper began to overheat in the judge's hands. "We consider the Devil to be guilty of several minor offences, for which the ancillary penalties envisaged by the code... And lastly the request made by the defence to condemn God for slander is rejected…"."

"An arbitration verdict," said the lawyer.

The typewritten document burst into flames in the judge's hands and the flames rapidly devoured human justice. However, nobody was capable of feeling surprised at this point. Tom Salomon gestured to the guards, who freed Satan from his cell, and the handcuffs around his wrists were unlocked, allowing him to taste the pleasant feeling of freedom.

In spite of all the excitement going on at the benches, the demon approached his lawyer to shake his hand, overwhelmed by the photographers and their flashing cameras, "I owe the rest of eternity to you, Mr Valance".

"Man of little faith," Nick joked.

Making his way through the crowd, Bernard Louis also came over to the defence lawyer.

"My compliments, Mr Valance," he said, clenching his teeth, "but this is not the end: I'm going to appeal to the Supreme Court and to God's judgement if necessary. Your client will not go unpunished."

"God is directly involved in this matter," the lawyer objected, "it is an intolerable conflict of interests."

Natalie Brinne also approached the defence table. "You did amazingly well, Nick... really. But I fear that this will mark the end of my career".

"My law firm needs new associates," he suggested, with a smile, "what do you say if we discuss it over dinner?"

When the judge declared the hearing closed, a black crow was seen fluttering around in the air and Lucifer recognized it: it was Puck. Then he noticed a woman with red hair in the crowd at the back of the room: Bensoria's long hair moved around to greet him.

In his office, the furious attorney general, Erik Marduk, hurled the bottle of liqueur against the television screen and it exploded, giving out a thousand sparks. He took the phone off the hook and gulped his drink down avidly. Later on, he planned to declare how proud he was of his substitutes, who had faced a superhuman enemy, but right now he was beginning to taste the most humiliating failure of his career.

The news of Satan's release from prison was received with great enthusiasm in the depths of Hell, where wild celebrations began to take place in the various circles of hell. The angel Camiel also performed a series of spins and twirls in the skies above Zurich.

The members of the jury were interviewed as they left the courtroom.

"Of course we couldn't incriminate God," the president explained, "but nevertheless we realized that there was no substantial evidence against the accused and therefore his acquittal was the only choice."

"This is an extremely dangerous precedent," Bernard Louis commented. "After this verdict, any criminal could be acquitted. The law does not exist anymore: by absolving evil and the premise that it exists, the law has condemned itself."

The imam added his contribution. "It will not be easy for another opportunity like this one to occur. Human law has demonstrated its limits to all".

Yorgo Mirakis could not hold back his joy. "We have always worshipped the Devil because we knew that he was good. Now, human justice has confirmed that".

Von Hugh also gave his opinion. "It is a symbolic sentence: it is as if man, by forgiving the ancient tempter, had symbolically forgiven himself for having given up the Garden of Eden. The feelings of guilt have been exorcised, and not with an expiatory sacrifice, but with total and unconditional forgiveness".

Pope Teomondo maintained his self-control. "A serious sin has been committed today. Forgiving the Devil means becoming his accomplice. We must not be resigned."

When the accused looked out of the courtroom, wrapped in a black coat, the journalists assailed him.

Overwhelmed by the flashing cameras, he put on a pair of dark glasses and tried to move away, escorted by the UN Blue Helmets, towards the exit, where a group of Satanists were waiting for him.

"It's all the lawyers' fault," father Cimor declared, appearing suddenly next to Nick Valance in the corridor of the courthouse. He was still walking with a stick. "Now millions of people all over the world will not know what to protect themselves from anymore."

"It's only a trial," Nick said, trying to play down the situation.

"But having eliminated the fear of God and trampling on his authority will only lead to a rebellion and you will be responsible for it!" He lifted his walking stick with a prophetic air, not noticing that he was at the top of a flight of steps. For a moment, his eyes met Satan's eyes at the end of the corridor, and his sneering smile made Cimor lose his balance. Cimor felt himself waver precariously on the edge of the staircase for a few seconds, as if an invisible hand were holding him, but then he fell.

Nick was unable to stop him: he rolled noisily down the flight of steps until he reached the lower landing.

When judge Tom Salomon left the courtroom later on, thanking the heavens that he was still alive, the corridors had partially emptied. He noticed Nick Valance standing near the lifts.

"So, in the end you actually did it, Mr Valance," he said, with a faint smile. *Fiat iustitia et pereat mundus…* In order to do justice, we judged and condemned the whole world, including God."

"Basically, the law was true to itself," Valance said. "Nobody can be *legibus solutus*, above the law, not even the legislator."

The old magistrate took the grey wig off his head. "Next week I'm going to apply for my pension. This conclusion to my career has made me suffer".

"I'm sorry, sir, but you've ended your career with a flourish: you managed the trial splendidly."

"You never made a stand, Valance, but now that it's all over, you can tell me. Are you religious or an atheist?"

"Oh," Nick shrugged, "sometimes it depends on my client."

21

The risen angel

<blockquote>
The LORD saw it, and it displeased him that there was no justice.

Isaiah 59:15
</blockquote>

With torches, crosses and metal bars, numerous millenarian worshippers had met in the Kantonales Gerichtsgebäude square, ready to correct the unjust verdict and the police had been deployed to defend the building.

On the balcony of the town hall, the American and Russian presidents were staring silently at the sight of the people running around down below. The green waters of the Limmat river shone with the reflections of the fires burning along its banks; the richest democracy in the world appeared to be on its knees, evidently in the grip of a possession.

We must acknowledge the situation... there is no longer black and white... We are all becoming grey," said the Russian president.

The American president did not reply.

The French president cheerfully joined them, uncorking a bottle of champagne. "The law has surpassed itself! With this sentence nobody will be able to accuse us of intolerance".

The other two looked at him.

Behind him, chancellor König approached. "You provoked all this! You played with fire and you have caused the whole world to burn!"

"I have ensured our re-election," Renard replied, in his defence.

Without adding another word, the chancellor grabbed him by the throat and threw him to the floor.

"Hey, what are you doing?" Renard grunted, struggling to free himself.

The other man refused to let go.

It was the Russian and the American who reluctantly intervened: they lifted the aggressor and pulled him off the Frenchman.

Renard sat down on an armchair, massaging his neck.

"I'm not made for physical disputes…," he admitted. Then, noticing the hostile looks he was receiving, he adjusted his tie with a reassuring air. "But let's look at the positive sides, gentlemen. We will have the Satanists' votes!"

಄ ಄ ಄

With the precision of a surgeon, the hired assassin got the gunsight into focus. On the slightly sloping roof of the Kunsthaus, the art museum in front of the courthouse, his silhouette lay motionless in the rain. Through the lens, he observed the people coming out of the building - the journalists, the police, the Satanists - until finally he identified his target.

Drying his forehead, he took aim. It was his umpteenth attack, but he felt nervous, like a beginner. In front of him, Lucifer was in clear view and vulnerable. A silver bullet was ready in the barrel of the gun.

He had been handsomely paid for this job and had been promised impunity and a one-way ticket to a paradise in the Pacific. The chance of a lifetime.

The angel Camiel was flying over the area when she spotted the outline of the armed man on top of the museum and sensed what was happening. It had been forbidden to intervene in human matters, especially after her testimony at the trial, but her former lover's life was in danger. She had a couple of seconds to decide whether to sacrifice perfection or let Lucifer be murdered, a difficult choice for a being who was used to reasoning with all the time in eternity. His salvation would be her damnation, but perhaps they would find themselves again in the fires of Hell.

A tear of nostalgia fell from her eyes and was carried away by the wind. Camiel knew that he was no longer the same Lucifer that she had loved and the fear of losing the memory of her love made her hesitate.

The rain continued to fall and the angel concentrated, as Lucifer had taught her to do, and let the light within her uncontrollably gush out. A dazzling glare, an intense and vivid light, left the angel's body, lighting up the roof of the building. For the first time since eternity, Camiel was able to shine with her own light, like a little star in the grey sky.

In the street, Yorgo Mirakis was trying to reach his prince, making his way through the crowd, when he saw the glare up above and, further ahead on the roof, an outline with a strange reflection that caught his attention: a mirror or the lens of a gunsight.

He sensed the danger and yelled, "There's an assassin!"

The hired assassin was aiming between the Devil's horns with his finger on the trigger. Mirakis desperately threw himself towards the Devil, pushing and shoving through the human barrier. The assassin's finger pulled on the trigger and the Satanist's voice was lost in the general commotion. Only Lucifer heard it faintly. A faint *click* and the bullet left the gun silently as Yorgo reached Lucifer. It cut through the air, invisible to all, while the Satanist pushed his master away, plunging a short distance away from the target.

An explosion and a spurt of blood scared everyone present. The crowd opened up, screaming around the victim, while someone pointed at the roof of the building and the Luciferans threw themselves onto Satan's bloody body to protect him. The assassin swore, reloading his gun and taking aim again. Lucifer got up and saw the man who worshipped him lying next to him with his chest stained with blood; he couldn't believe that one day he would be in debt to him.

"Prince, I'm dying…," Yorgo wheezed .

He grabbed his hand.

"Don't worry. Today you will be with me in Hell."

A grateful smile and a tear trickled down behind the man's dark glasses.

On the roof of the building, the hired assassin was preparing to open fire again, but a sudden fog had come down on the Hirschengraben. As the man tried to identify the victim, something sharp poked him in the neck. The killer turned and froze before the unimaginable.

Dressed like a medieval executioner, with a wide tunic and a black hood, Barbatos threatened him with a pitchfork.

"If you pull that trigger I will burn you personally," he bellowed, foaming at the mouth. "And I *will pierce* every part of your body with my pitchfork."

The assassin was unable to understand the whole sentence: the hair on his head stood up on end and he yelled with a voice he didn't recognize, before fleeing in terror.

He could hear Barbatos's s course laughter behind him, accompanying him for a long time as he ran.

In the sky, the angel Camiel smiled: Lucifer was safe and so was her perfection.

Fluttering with her soft wings, she approached the road until the rebel angel noticed her. They exchanged a look of indefinable nostalgia; a ray of sun had crossed their hell.

Then, timidly, Camiel took flight again and gradually disappeared beyond the clouds.

∽ ∽ ∽

Because of the bad weather that had caused a blackout in the entire city, the news was spreading uncontrollably: people were saying that God was dead, that the Devil had been raised to the heavens, that other angels had rebelled. The Swiss Guard had come from the Vatican for father Cimor, who was bruised after falling down the stairs, and had taken him to a safe place.

Sheltering from the heavy rain under the porticoes, the prince of demons walked in silence. His wet hair lined his face and the noise of the heavy rain covered the sound of his footsteps. He had gone back inside the building, towards the back entrance, and had stopped in the courtyard. The world was not ready for him. He took off his coat and went into the middle of the courtyard where he was soaked by the silvery splashes of the rain. He opened his large wings and looked up at the sky with his arms open.

"The serpent lives on," he shouted, and the sky replied with a rumble.

Then an unusual glare formed high up above him and a light with a human form, but a superhuman essence, descended, flapping its wings.

"*Jibra'il…*," Lucifer murmured, extending his claws.

In a few moments the light became stronger and an angelic figure appeared, with a halo floating above a head of curly hair.

"I come to bring you a message from the Almighty," said the archangel Gabriel, as he landed on the ground. "The Lord is disappointed in the way the humans have behaved. However, in his infinite mercy, he will grant them an extension, another fragment of eternity, so that they can change and become what He wishes them to be."

"They will not change. Humans feel what I feel and desire just like I desire. If *Jhwh* wants servants, he will have to start all over again, from the beginning."

"That's what will happen!" Gabriel threatened.

Lucifer heard more flapping of wings behind him and noticed another angel with jet black hair and a proud look in his eyes.

"You are just an unwanted guest."

"*Mika'il…*"

The ancient rival who had opposed his revolt, the most faithful and brave of God's angels, Michael, was standing there before him. They had fought each other thousands of years before on the clouds and their battle had slowed down the advance of the rebels, allowing the celestial powers to organize their defence.

The memories, sounds, images of the war that had cost him Heaven seemed to come to life in the square, vivid and real like in the Devil's nightmares. The boundless plain of the sky above the clouds filled with impenetrable squadrons, shining tanks, winged horses; and the battle that exploded, causing hell to emerge in the sky, with the swords of Lucifer and Michael as they crossed each other, surrounded by lightning bolts, the rumble of thunder and arrows of light. Finally Lucifer saw his front line broken and the imminence of defeat and decided to aim for the Seventh Heaven, attempting a solitary, desperate forward assault. But at that point, God was there, invincible, ready to face him with his thunderbolts.

"Do not exult before the Almighty!" Michael said, shattering the vision. "The unmentionable one had envisaged this conclusion to the trial... it was part of his inscrutable design."

Lucifer smiled scornfully. "An old alibi."

The angels of God stood next to each other and the Devil's dark figure passed between them, as he slowly walked away.

∽ ∽ ∽

In the deserted entrance hall of the courthouse, which was lit up by a yellowish light pouring in from the windows high up, a woman was waiting in silence. Lucifer and Sophia looked at each other for a long time without speaking, as if the barriers of time had collapsed around them. Contemplating her, he remembered her beauty from so many centuries before, when he had loved her in the shade of a walnut tree.

"Perhaps I should write about you," Sophia whispered, trying to hide her inner turmoil. "The world has a right to know and to get to know you the way I know you."

The devil moved closer to her and touched her lips with his finger. "Sometimes we need to be silent if we want to be heard."

She didn't answer. There were no words to express her feelings. The only thing she could hear in her mind was the hammering sound of her heart, a heart that she felt did not belong only to her.

"You haven't told me what I was like in my previous life."

"Brave, generous, sweet… and almost as beautiful as you are now."

A gust of wind dried up his words and the *kamsin*, the desert wind, blew on through the entrance hall.

Satan lightly touched her wet hair, caressed her hips and her tummy, until his sensitive nails stopped, as he perceived a weak but rhythmic clandestine heartbeat. A tremor ran through the demon's body, a rare and beautiful sensation to repress in his empty chest.

It was him: his son.

The son of Satan, the Antichrist, had been conceived. After a long wait, the ancient prophecy of his coming was destined to come true. As it is written, *he*, his son, would be raised to rule the world, seducing peoples and nations like a new prophet and, on Judgment Day, he would fight alongside his father, against God and against the son of God, to create new disorder.

"Take care of yourself, Satia," said a voice that it seemed to emerge with difficulty. "I will be away, but I fear that you will not forget me."

The demon's shadow slowly began to appear on the floor, gradually becoming more substantial. Lucifer did not look like a devil anymore but he had become an angel again, the rebel angel that he had once been. Deep in his eyes, Sophia could see the abyss from which he had re-emerged.

"One day you will fly again," she said.

A gust of wind shook the building and several windows shattered up above, causing glass to rain down all around. Opening his wings, Lucifer wrapped himself around Sophia's body.

"A kind of magic," he said.

Then he pulled back his wings. He smiled and moved towards the exit, without turning back. The vast ocean of eternity was about to separate them again. He could hear, inside himself, Satia's cries on the stake, as she was enveloped in flames.

She watched him disappear beyond the portico, as the clear dark shadow reached him, getting bigger and bigger.

"I will wait for you until the end of time," she thought, "and I will find you again."

Without the Devil, her life would have been a living hell.

∽ ∽ ∽

The rain continued to beat down on the building, as Nick Valance appeared at the back portico, cautiously looking around. He saw the flooded roads, a few tiny figures of people running in the distance and no taxis: this evening was not a quiet one.

A figure in the colonnade caught his attention and it looked like his client. He walked over to him, shaken by the gusts of wind, but no one was there; a little further on, the courthouse car park was deserted.

"Thank you, Mr Valance," Satan said, suddenly appearing behind him.

"Oh… are you looking for a taxi too?" Nick exclaimed.

"I doubt that they would take me all the way home," he replied, smiling ambiguously. "Now do you believe that I exist, man?"

"I still have some doubts."

"Well, lawyers will always be able to find a job down there."

Some shouting in the distance caught their attention: the two factions, of good and evil, were fighting in the city and it was impossible to distinguish them.

"Perhaps God has already lost," Lucifer commented, twisting the tip of his black goatee beard. "The moment he created the first prohibition, the moment he felt the need to create a prohibition, he began to lose."

Standing with his head held high, he seemed to be supporting the sky with his horns.

"Will there be any changes in the world now?" the lawyer asked, lifting his collar.

"Nothing will change. They'll say that the trial was an imposture, a propaganda stunt, that we were all acting, and it will soon be forgotten."

The lawyer was not surprised by that prospect.

"As far as the question you are about to ask is concerned, Mr Valance, we will know that on the last day."

"What?" Nick asked, astonished.

"You were wondering if justice had been done," he said, as little flashes of light flickered in his eyes.

Valance didn't ask any other questions and they remained silent for a few minutes, like old friends, watching the rain as it fell in sheets all around. When dawn approached and the rain had slowed down, a timid sunrise began to light up the sky to the east. Some order needed to be restored in the city; the next day was Sunday, a sacred day for football supporters, and some preparation was needed.

With a sudden screeching of tyres on the ground, an old Bentley entered the square. After diving around it a couple of times, it stopped in front of the portico and two individuals got out.

"We've found you," a blond youth said, dressed in an eccentric-looking long loose dressing-gown. The other man, wearing a dark cloak and with a cigar between his teeth, grumbled something unintelligible.

"Asmodeus, Astaroth!" Lucifer said, looking pleased: "Happy to see you both again." The hugs in the rain were accompanied by roaring noises. Then Satan introduced them all. "This is the devil's advocate! And these are two of my trusty archons".

"His reputation has descended to the underworld," Astoroth said, complimenting him, offering Valance his clawed hand, which Valance took awkwardly.

Asmodeus bowed low.

The howling of dogs coming from the car was calling them. Through the darkened windows, Nick could make out the shape of a strange animal.

Barbatos, who was driving, opened the door to let out the wild beast that was fidgeting around inside the car: a black dog, much larger than the car could possibly hold, with three snarling heads.

"Cerberus!" Lucifer exclaimed.

With the three heads barking in chorus, the dog jumped up at his master. Valance stepped back.

The dog of the Underworld, the Beast of ancient mythology, was a few steps away from him, alive and real, and he was licking his master with three tongues.

A few bolts of lightning struck the square not far away from them, making Astaroth's ears stand up. "We are vulnerable here, we should go."

Satan turned to Nick. "We must say goodbye, man. Hoping not to see each other again".

"Bon voyage," he replied with a nod of his head.

Barbatos's car made an awkward manoeuvre and hit a lamppost.

"I noticed that you addressed me *informally…*," the prince said, walking away.

"The trial is over, Satan, you're not my client anymore."

The Devil stopped in the middle of the street and their eyes met through the falling rain.

"My name is Lucifer," he said.

Then he turned and caught up with the others.

The lawyer watched him get into the car and drive away through the deserted streets, until he could no longer read the number plate STN 666.

The mysterious charmer had gone, disappearing into the oblivion of the night, leaving behind just a slight whiff of sulphur, the invisible sign of an unreal presence.

The rain continued to pour. Nick was soaked and tired and his wife was undoubtedly expecting him back in London. He lowered his hat over his eyes, opened his umbrella and headed home.

Famous quotes

It is impossible to mention all the sources consulted during the preparation of this book, but following are a few maxims and famous quotes that contributed to inspiring some of the "diabolic" reasoning.

The finest trick of the devil is to persuade you that he does not exist.

Charles Baudelaire

In hell the devil is a positive hero

Stanislaw Jerzy Lec

I believe that our Heavenly Father invented man because he was disappointed in the monkey. After that he gave up on other experiments.

Mark Twain

God is dead. He left us two Testaments.

Heinrich Weisner

The God of the Christians is a father who makes much of his apples, and very little of his children.

Denis Diderot

We owe everything we know to Satan and to his smuggled apples.

Henry Louis Mencken

If God knew in advance the sins of which man would be guilty, He was clearly responsible for all the consequences of those sins when He decided to create man.

Bertrand Russell

It was God himself, who at the end of his day's work lay down as a serpent under the tree of knowledge: thus he recuperated from being God. / The Devil is simply God's idleness on that seventh day.

The devil has the widest perspective for God; that's why he keeps himself so far away from Him - for the devil is the oldest friend of knowledge.

Where the tree of knowledge stands is always paradise: that's what the oldest and the most recent serpents declare.

When asses are needed. - You will not get the crowd to cry Hosanna until you ride into town on an ass.

And they did not know how to love their God except by crucifying man.

It is your innocence not to know what innocence is.

One repays a teacher badly if one always remains nothing but a pupil.

Friedrich Nietzsche

Everything lives because it is opposed to something. I am the one to whom everything is opposed. But if I did not exist, nothing would exist.

I am the absolute negative, the embodiment of nothingness. What you desire and cannot be obtained, what you dream of because it cannot exist.

I am the lunar master of all dreams, the solemn musician of all silences... I am the one you have always sought and will never be able to find.

Fernando Pessoa

Angels can fly because they can take themselves lightly.

Gilbert Keith Chesterton

∞ ∞ ∞

Finito di stampare nel mese di Giugno 2018
per conto di Youcanprint *Self-Publishing*

* 9 7 8 8 8 2 7 8 3 1 6 6 3 *